SHAKES
BOOK ONE OF MURPHY'S LAWLESS

Mike Massa

Beyond Terra Press
Virginia Beach, VA

Copyright © 2020 by Mike Massa.

All rights reserved. No part of this publication may be reproduced, distributed or transmitted in any form or by any means, including photocopying, recording, or other electronic or mechanical methods, without the prior written permission of the publisher, except in the case of brief quotations embodied in critical reviews and certain other noncommercial uses permitted by copyright law. For permission requests, write to the publisher, addressed "Attention: Permissions Coordinator," at the address below.

Chris Kennedy/Beyond Terra Press
2052 Bierce Dr.
Virginia Beach, VA 23454
http://chriskennedypublishing.com/

Publisher's Note: This is a work of fiction. Names, characters, places, and incidents are a product of the author's imagination. Locales and public names are sometimes used for atmospheric purposes. Any resemblance to actual people, living or dead, or to businesses, companies, events, institutions, or locales is completely coincidental.

Cover Design by J Caleb Design.

Ordering Information:
Quantity sales. Special discounts are available on quantity purchases by corporations, associations, and others. For details, contact the "Special Sales Department" at the address above.

Shakes/Mike Massa -- 1st ed.
ISBN: 978-1950420995

For everyone who has ever made a drop far, far from home and found themselves wondering, even if only for an instant, just how the hell they got there.

Prelude

by Charles E. Gannon

Chapter One
Murphy

The Blackhawk banked, giving Murphy his last glimpse of Somalia. It was a mostly brown and tan expanse except for two dark epicenters of activity. The smaller of the two was home to the runways and tarmac above which they were rapidly rising. Around it was a gridwork of tents. Around those were angular defenses backed by outward-facing, Matchbox-sized vehicles and tiny figures. That was the American base in-theater. Other, smaller compounds were scattered around the city, more ragged but roughly analogous.

However, even the least orderly of those compounds were punctiliously arranged marvels compared to the far larger smudge at their approximate center, the smudge that marred the otherwise unexceptionedl desert waste palette: Mogadishu—a sprawling, chaotic jumble of low, sunbaked buildings, tin-roofed shacks, and every other conceivable kind of rudimentary shelter. At the lowest end of the survival spectrum, he saw blue plastic hurricane tarps unevenly lashed to the sheared and crumbling walls of long abandoned colonial ruins, desperate havens from the punishing sun.

"Good riddance," breathed Melissa "Missy" Katano as she leaned sharply inboard, her nostrils pinched tight. You couldn't smell Mogadishu from up here, but it seemed that she wasn't willing to lean any closer than necessary to the source of the superheated stink.

She must have seen Murphy's small smile. "What? You like it here?"

He hadn't seen that question coming, so didn't have an answer ready. However, it was Murphy's good fortune that Dr. Hampson was there to lean over and observe in an almost fatherly tone, "Well sometimes, no matter how unpleasant a place might be, we don't want to leave all of it—or what we experienced there—behind."

The one SEAL on the chopper, who was going home after having had his tour extended twice, glanced over at the unexpected interjection by the doctor. He glanced briefly at Murphy, then turned his gaze back out the other open door, eyes fixed upon the broad, blue expanse of the Indian Ocean and the thin sprinkling of fishing boats upon it.

Murphy managed not to frown. Doc Hampson meant well, but every once in a while, his deep civilian roots showed through. Like in this case. Sent in-country to look at the head wounds of a congresswoman's son, he had done something that few military doctors were likely to do: stop by to take a quick look at a much less urgent case that was puzzling the base's medicos.

It was the case of one Rodger Y. Murphy, U.S. Army, a hotshot young major who had experienced some mild unsteadiness in the wake of being a few meters too close to an improvised explosive device. He hadn't been close enough to be significantly roughed up by it. There were no concussion or open wounds, even though there were plenty of contusions on hands, knees, and back where the shockwave had rolled him in the dust along Mogadishu's Maxud Harbi Street. The young medics were trying to figure out why the young major still had lingering difficulties when he tried to type a report or clean a weapon.

But Dr. Hampson looked at him for all of three minutes, leaned back, and pronounced the diagnosis that was also a life sentence. "Multiple sclerosis," Hampson had said frankly. "No question about it. Well, not much question, but if you conduct the standard battery, I think that's what you're going to find."

Which, of course, the medicos had no reason to suspect. What with shock trauma in a combat zone and no history of the disease, it was a million-to-one that Major Murphy was suffering the onset of an unlooked-for disease instead of after-effects of the trauma. Doctors with five times their experience would have been just as likely to misdiagnose.

Then again, there weren't a whole lot of doctors of Robert Hampson's caliber. Not in the whole world, and not when it came down to brain and neurological diagnosis and treatment. After Hampson had trundled out of the ward with his perennial good humor, the young medicos had clustered near Murphy's end of the ward, trading muttered reports about what they knew of the specialist. To hear them talk, he was either the elect of God or a deity himself when it came to nerves or the brain.

The doc was also a good guy—sometimes too good, Murphy reflected as the heavily built man leaned back into his seat, eclipsing a small, spare soldier seated on his other side. Hampson's reflex had been pure civvy: jumping into a conversation to help out a startled or rattled pal. But here, in this chopper, it wasn't a civilian world. It was a world of fighters and the people who worked with them. People who took care of themselves.

Of all of them, Katano was the closest to civilian, but she'd been in-country so long—trying to keep all the allies working on the same page, and supply and logistics flowing without completely ditching protocol—that she had almost as hard an edge as the soldiers and airmen and sailors she dealt with.

The rest of the compartment was filled with other weary faces that were just waiting out another ride in a shuddering Blackhawk. The SEAL officer was the size of a bear, but his young face was already seamed by lines that most people wouldn't acquire until well into their thirties. Next to him was a blue-eyed, sunburned guy wearing a flight suit, a pilot's wings, and a hastily reattached captain's patch. Another guy, about the same age, was sitting just beyond the flight engineer/chief, wearing a hundred-yard stare instead of a rank patch, his face faintly dark with deep-driven grit except for a raccoon mask of paleness around his eyes. Definitely a cav officer who'd spent a lot of time driving around looking for UN-baiting bandits and bad guys—who were often the same thing.

Their collective stillness was offset by the middle-aged man on Murphy's side of the fuselage, wearing well-worn tactical gear and clothes to match. No signs of rank or service branch. Defense contractor rep? Smuggler? Private security? Spook? No, Murphy revised, not a spook: way too jumpy, even for an analyst thrown into the field.

The fellow leaned forward and shouted over the rotors toward the cockpit. "Hey, how much longer?"

The pilot glanced at her copilot, whose hands were already more firmly locked on the controls. "Who wants to know?" the pilot shouted back.

"An American citizen," the guy answered loudly, a little more testy.

"Well then, John Q. Public, it's like your momma said when you were in the back of that hot station wagon: we'll get there when we get there." She turned to face the plexiglass cockpit.

John Q. Public sputtered, striving for a retort as the passenger beside him—another guy in sanitized tactical dress—shook his head and tilted a slow, almost sleepy smile at him. "Not worth it, friend."

Mr. Citizen glanced at the man—whose eyes hardened slightly—then shrugged and slumped back in his seat.

The still-smiling fellow turned toward Murphy. Almost every pair of eyes in this damned country measured you, assessed you, but these were different. His assessment seemed professional. Like an interrogator's. Or a cop's.

What he said didn't give any clues about his origins. "You look like you're going back to the world."

"So do you."

"That's 'cause I am." The man's smile widened before it faded. "For now." And he waited.

Murphy kept the frown off his face. Kept the annoyance off, too. Annoyance at himself for no longer being able to instantly access the stockpile of bullshit responses, empty remarks, and harmless comebacks that he'd picked up ever since ROTC, fourteen years and several lifetimes ago. The MS—the ever-present fear of it—had taken that from him, too.

And the guy saw it. A slight frown, the kind when a person encounters a conversational twist they didn't expect, a break or a flaw they hadn't foreseen. His eyes simultaneously became slightly more wary but also slightly more compassionate. And in that instant, Murphy saw what he hated to see most of all: a shift to pity.

Damn it: no. "I'm just glad to be going—"

The Blackhawk shifted; not a thermal, a small, sharp banking maneuver. "Hold on," the pilot shouted over her shoulder.

"Trouble?" asked the copilot in way too calm a voice.

"Not sure. Dye in the water. Ours. Near that raft." Her copilot glanced over. "We've got orders—"

"Can't ignore the dye. SOP."

"But the VIP—"

"Enough." The pilot's voice was sharper. "My bird, my call." She craned her neck.

The copilot did as well. "Yeah, that's one of ours down there in the—"

"That's one of our *uniforms*," the pilot emphasized. "Doesn't tell us who's wearing it. Zipper," she called back at her crew chief, "get eyes-on while I come around. Too many boats out here. We've gotta watch for—"

"Launch plume!" yelled Zipper. "Eight o'clo—!"

He never finished; the pilot's sharp evasive maneuver threw him back from the door into the passenger compartment.

"Lieutenant, eyes on the other side. I need to know if—"

"Captain," shouted the copilot—too loud and too panicked to be anything but a complete newb—"Bigger plume. Coming up from the trawler at our—"

The threat warning system began to wail. The Blackhawk's engines screamed as the pilot pulled it into what felt like a counter-banking maneuver so steep that Murphy would have sworn they were going backward—

A flash. A blast that blew his ability to hear right out of his head. Pieces of the craft spraying up and out from where the copilot's seat should have been. Some of the eyes around him were wide, others narrowed and alert as the Blackhawk seemed to both roll and pitch forward, as if the tail was coming over the nose…

Chest hard against his straps, the guy with the raccoon mask sighed. "Ah, shit—"

And then there was nothing.

* * * * *

Chapter Two
Murphy Awakes

Murphy awoke with a start. Gray, utilitarian walls and lighting—although the lights were unusual, somehow. The air was canned: no doubt about it. And he was not lying, but reclining.

Careful now; maybe you've been captured—

"Take it easy, Major. You are safe and among friends."

English accent. Measured, the way medical personnel talk to people who may or may not be screwed up. Murphy struggled to rise up on his elbows. He felt slightly weak, had a momentary wash of vertigo, then the world righted.

Two men were seated at the end and to either side of where he lay, which from his angle looked like a cross between a sick bay bed and a gurney. Labels were in English. They were both in what looked kind of like flight suits, but more bulky and more substantial. There were no markings on either.

Not enough information to make any assumptions either way—which wouldn't have been safe or wise to do anyway. So he said, "Murphy. Rodger Y.; Major, U.S. Army. Serial number 984—"

The two men—both tall, but one much older than the other—smiled. The older and thinner one waved a hand. "Yes. We know. In fact, my companion here—let's call him Mr. Nephew—is still a reservist in your military. Different branch, however."

Mr. Nephew reminded Murphy of the SEAL in the chopper, but whereas that guy was a bear, this one was more a tiger: a little taller and leaner. But Murphy's intended query—an attempt to sniff out if he really was affiliated with the U.S. military—died in his throat as memory rose up. "The Blackhawk. What—?"

Mr. Nephew nodded. "Went down in the Indian Ocean. November 17, 1993. Copilot and crew chief were KIA, although the copilot's body was never found. The pilot and passengers survived."

Murphy frowned. "How? And why? Hell, the second missile wasn't an RPG round; it was homing on us and made a contact hit. The front half of the chopper should have been gone—and me with it."

"As best we can tell, the second missile's warhead was defective. Went off late and weak. Damage to the cockpit—and the copilot—was essentially from the impact. That's why the pilot and everyone else close survived."

Murphy did not even nod. No falling into the trap of routine or casual exchanges. Hell, his training was to not communicate at all. But if these guys were working for hajis—No; something was off, but not something as simple as that. If this was theater, a bid to get him to believe himself in safe hands, then it was all at once way too good and way too amateurish.

The two guys, particularly the big one, emitted service vibe as strong as he'd ever felt. And not service as pogues; these guys had been in the shit. And that was damn near impossible to fake. Just like the accents: they were too damned good. The older one was speaking in that kind of controlled cant of the Brits—King's English, he'd heard it called—and the other had just enough of a twang that Murphy guessed he was from the mid-Atlantic states, probably Virginia or Maryland, possibly Delaware.

But if these guys were impostors trying to inveigle his trust, then why were they such amateurs about uniforms? Their weird flight suits weren't in anyone's inventory, and they just looked wrong. Flight suits were fitted out with the kinds of loops and fasteners that you'd need in a plane; fatigues for ground pounders had buttons not zippers, more pockets in different places, and more places to hang or attach gear. Their suits had both—sorta—but also a number of flaps that didn't make sense, as well as what looked like sealable collars and cuffs.

And why no rank patches, no national or service branch insignias? Okay, so maybe they were playing the "intel neutral" game, but still, that was usually done by covering things up or removing velcroed patches. These suits looked like they had never had either affixed.

So how was it they were so good at the vibe and the language, and so bad at the costuming? It didn't make any sense. Unless they weren't trying to put on an act, which made even less sense. And was a whole lot more creepy, if true.

And another thing—"You read out the whole date of the attack on us, year and all. Why?" He paused, ditching the prohibition against talking; it was more important to learn what was going on. "So, are we being recorded? Is this a—a sanitized debrief? Who are you guys with?"

Mr. Nephew smiled slightly, shook his head. "We are not being recorded, although come to think of it, that might have been a good idea. And if anyone is providing debrief information, it's not you conveying it to us: it's we who have to convey it to you."

"Huh? What the hell do you mean?"

The tiger-guy's smile widened. "I'll let my colleague—Mr. Nuncle—explain."

"Captain Murphy, we mentioned the precise date of your crash because you've been unconscious for a while."

"Then why am I still in the same fatigues?" He could even smell the same heat-brewed body odor, but he wasn't going to mention that. Come to think of it, he could also smell a faint salt-water tang as well... "Wait a minute, you didn't even bother to change my clothes when you fished me out of the ocean?"

Mr. Nuncle held up a helpless hand. "We most certainly would have. But we were not the ones who recovered you."

There was something in the older guy's voice and the younger guy's reaction that spiked Murphy's wariness meter. For the first time, they grew slightly tense—just a moment, and just a shade of it—but it had been there. "Okay, what aren't you telling me?" *Wait: the date.* "This has something to do with the date of the crash."

The older guy frowned sadly; his face got longer and a little older looking. "You are to be congratulated on your conjecture, Major Murphy. Our recounting of the date is indeed central to what you must learn about what has happened to you."

Murphy responded to the sudden chill of fear by heading straight at its source. "Then spit it out: why is the date so important?"

Mr. Nephew's eyes did not blink as they sought his. "Because it's not that date anymore. Not even close."

Murphy kept pushing toward the center of the growing terror. "Stop the theatrics. What's the date?"

"August. 2125."

Murphy shunted his burgeoning terror into outraged facetiousness. "Okay, guys. I don't know who you are, or who put you up to this, but this is a pretty shitty joke. I mean, maybe if we hadn't lost someone on the chopper, it would be okay, but it's lousy to build a practical joke on the copilot's grave, because that's pretty much what you're doing here."

"You're right," Tiger-Nephew said with a slow nod. "That would be a shitty joke. But this isn't a joke."

Murphy had been watching their eyes. They were somber, even sad. They didn't check their performances against each other, nor were they so rigidly focused on the act that it caused an unnatural sense of timing or predetermined intent. Unless, that is, it wasn't an act—"No," Murphy rebutted, surging forward, "this is all bullshit. Weirdest damn strategy for producing POW disorientation I've ever heard of, but it isn't going to work. It's too freaking ridiculous."

Mr. Nuncle sighed, rose. "We presumed you would have that reaction. We'd probably have the same one, put in your place. That is why we're going to let you spend as long as you need with someone from your time. He even served in your theater of operations—Somalia—albeit a few years later."

The heavy bulkhead door slid aside—just like in old reruns of *Star Trek*—and a new guy walked in, saluting the two already in the room. He wore a uniform Murphy recognized. Pararescue jumper. Lieutenant. A little younger than Murphy. He saluted as he introduced himself. "Ike Franklin, Major Murphy. Nice to meet you, sir. Wish it was under better—well, sane—circumstances."

Time to blow their cover, whatever game they might be playing. "Nice try. Uniform is a complete match. Accent is perfect. You guys have done your homework well. Or are you working for some rogue cell? Is that it?"

The new guy sighed. "I get it, Major, I really do. Those of us who had higher clearances wondered the same thing when we were awakened: was this some elaborate mind game to disorient us, get us to drop classified information? And you know what we figured out?"

Murphy shook his head, swallowed. The guy who called himself Franklin seemed so natural, so genuine, that Murphy's worst fears—no matter how irrational—were growing. "No. What did you figure out?"

"That none of us knew anything important enough to warrant all of this." The guy in the pararescue fatigues waved a broad hand to take in the whole compartment. "Tell me, Major. Just what do you know that would make an enemy willing to put on this kind of crazy show? I'm familiar with the info that is dished out at your rank, probably heard a lot of the same material since I served roughly during those years. I heard it because we might have to make snap decisions having to do with wounded personnel with sensitive intel. So I know most of the same sensitive data points about nukes, particularly small ones. I'm also guessing we both know a bit about comm protocols that probably never made it online, at least not where Netscape could find it."

Murphy blinked. There was something about the casualness with which he said, "Netscape"...

"But at the end of the day, you know how it goes: the services are full of folks from O-3 to O-5 who have a gambling habit, a drug habit, a sex habit, or alimony payments to beat the band. Those are the folks who are spilling the semi-secrets, not us—and for pennies on the dollar, compared to what it would cost to set up something like this."

Murphy struggled to find something to say, some brash counterpoint to which he could affix his flagging defiance and courage—but nothing showed up. His well of snappy comebacks was dry.

Mr. Nuncle rose, followed a moment later by Mr. Nephew, who said, "Sorry, Major. I really am. I've known several people who've had to grapple with this kind of one-way trip into the future. It's never easy, and the longer the time they've been gone, the harder it is. And you—well, you've been gone a very long time." He nodded and departed right behind Mr. Nuncle.

Murphy swallowed again, realized he was shaking slightly.

Franklin slid into the chair Mr. Nuncle had vacated and folded his hands. "Listen—"

"NO. *You* listen." Murphy clasped his hands to keep them still. "I don't buy this. Any of it. There's no way I could be in the future. That I could have—what? Slept through more than a century? That kind of technology—no one has, or had, it. Not even close."

Franklin shrugged. "You're right about that. But like the others said, our people weren't the ones who recovered you."

"So who did?"

Franklin leaned back and sighed. "You're not going to like or believe the answer, not at first."

"Of course I won't, because this is all bullshit. But tell me anyway—just for the entertainment value."

"Okay. You were abducted by aliens."

"By—?" And before he could stop himself, Murphy was laughing. Hysterically. Too loud and too wild, even to his own ears. Because if this wasn't an increasingly improbable charade...

"By aliens," Franklin repeated. "The same ones who grabbed me."

Murphy didn't immediately realize that he had stopped laughing, as if someone had turned off a switch. "What do you mean?"

"I mean just what I said, Major. Me and a buddy—Special Forces—we were as good as dead near the Ethiopian border in Somalia. Surrounded. No water, and not half a mag left between us. Then everything goes quiet. A few minutes later, a guy in shades and a suit walks up toward us and gives us the spiel a lot of us heard, 'You can come with me or you can die right here.' Not much of a choice. And we didn't know that going with him meant a one-way ride into the future. And even farther."

"Even farther?"

"Really? You haven't guessed by now? That we are nowhere near Earth?"

Murphy suppressed a shudder. "Go ahead: it's a good story. Lie to me some more."

Franklin shook his head, frustrated but smiling. "Major, you're one tough nut. Gonna be a real asset when you come around."

"Don't count on it."

Franklin's shrug was larger this time. "Suit yourself. The universe has got plenty of time. We're the ones who are playing beat the clock."

"And what does that mean?"

"It means that there's a reason you're being awakened at this place and at this time. It's because we're at war. Have been for a few years, now."

"At war with whom?"

"Well, as it turns out, with the same people who snatched us from Earth."

"Yeah, sure. So, tell me: are we fighting the greens or the grays?"

Franklin frowned. "Far as I know, there aren't any 'greens.' And the grays—if that's what they are—are on our side. Kinda."

Murphy was shaking inside but steeled himself to keep plunging forward, to get this impostor to finally show his hand, to reveal a crack in his act, a flaw in the story. "Okay. So why don't you tell me about the enemies who abducted me and the war and all the rest."

"That'll take a while."

"Well, according to you, I've got nothing but time."

Franklin smiled. "True, that." Then he leaned back and started to talk.

* * *

Murphy held up his hand. "Stop."

Franklin halted mid-word and squinted appraisingly at Murphy. "You look...uh, ill. Major."

"Nope," Murphy lied. "It's just a lot to take in."

Franklin smiled sympathetically. "Don't I know it."

Well, maybe you do and maybe you don't, Murphy retorted silently. But it sure did sound like he did. Franklin had answered every question not only with ease, but the kind of casual side commentary that you just didn't get in a constructed scenario. Frankly, not even the best spies on TV shows or in films demonstrated the unaffected, almost lazy inventiveness that Ike did. Which meant that it might not be invented. Which would mean that what he was saying was the truth.

Murphy once again had to clamp down the rising nausea. For a brief moment, he envied the contents of his stomach; at least they could escape. For Murphy, there was no leaving himself behind, no way to find the ejection seat if this was his new reality, slightly more than one hundred thirty years further along the timeline from the moment when he'd lost consciousness in the Blackhawk heading down toward the Indian Ocean. Which brought up an interesting glitch in the story of his "abduction," one that might prove to be the loose thread that would undo Franklin's tapestry of lies. "Wait a minute. You said that the abductors—the Kuh-torr—?"

"K-tor," Franklin corrected with a nod, eliding the syllables until they almost ran together.

"Yeah—you said that they gave you a choice. They spoke to you. Why not us?"

Franklin nodded—a casually confident gesture which made Murphy's hopeful stomach plummet. "That happened sometimes. For instance, some of the other abductees were on subs when their ticket was about to be punched. The Ktor intervened, but there wasn't the time for any chitchat. For them, like you, all they knew was that one moment they were expecting to be dead, the next they woke up safe and sound." Franklin's expression hardened. "Well, comparatively speaking. Not much safe about this new life. Not for us, anyhow."

"Not for us." No special emphasis, nor any theatrical de-emphasis. Just a conversational tone, a phrase like any other. *Jesus Christ, he's telling the truth. He really is.*

Murphy managed to turn his head before he threw up.

* * *

Franklin offered a second face towel. Murphy waved it away.

"Another glass of water?" the pararescue asked.

"No, thanks," Murphy coughed. "I'm good." Which was probably the biggest lie he'd ever told.

How they hell could he—or anyone—be "good" when their entire life was wiped away in an eyeblink? It was kind of the reverse of dying. Dying meant that you dropped out of everybody else's story, that you ceased to be. Which was terrifying. But this way, it was everybody else who dropped out of *your* story—leaving you as alone as any human had ever been. Family, friends, dreams went flitting past his mind's eye—and were gone, like vapor. Like they'd never existed. The nausea threatened again, but he choked it back down.

"We can stop now," Franklin said quietly, shifting in his chair as if he meant to get up in the direction of the hatch—if you could really call it that.

Murphy didn't respond. Did he want to stop? First, he'd wanted to disprove it all. Just now, he'd wanted to escape it. But the second after the desire to escape had passed, he knew—without even thinking—that there was nothing left but to go forward. *Yeah, but forward into what—?*

To hear Franklin tell it, he was now in a world which, about half a century after he left it, had slid into a crazy patchwork quilt of decline. Not what all the doomsday predictors had foreseen, either. Yeah, climate impact played a role, but before it could really roll out the huge effects that everyone had been talking about, simple human issues trumped them.

And even there, it wasn't what had been expected. It wasn't anything as simple as global overpopulation or famine. Because although the globe was more interconnected than ever, that didn't mean that a disaster in one region or at any given economic level turned into equally awful disasters in all the others. Instead, the bow wave of the crisis struck at coastal cities—well, megalopoli. Places like Manila and Rio and Lagos and Mumbai, where the services fell so far behind the urban influx, chaos, and crime, that cargo ships ultimately started avoiding them, urged along by Lloyds' refusal to insure any docking there.

That was the tipping point. Once cut off from sea-borne goods and supplies, the local population almost immediately became exponentially greater than those cities' carrying capacities. Unrest became revolt. Hunger became starvation. And crime lords became war lords.

Economies toppled. Refugees fled to the countryside, hoping to find a way to feed themselves. Others, paradoxically, collapsed upon the cities, the lure of jobs and services stronger than the fear of, or belief in, the decaying conditions there. Cities in the interior were swamped, drowned in the same wave of human desperation.

Currencies collapsed, followed by the governments that backed them. Coups pitted military juntas against crime syndicates that were almost as powerful as they were, and often came from the same backgrounds. Clean water, already in short supply, became the new currency in many places, along with canned food, medicines, and bullets.

And what had the rest of the world done? Less and less. Most of the Western powers that had the money and power to possibly—*possibly*—make a difference were also decried as opportunistic recolonizers. Voting publics in the West fretted and fought among themselves about what steps to take—but even if they had been able to make any productive plans, the situation deteriorated too rapidly for it to matter.

The other great powers? Russia was still attempting to sort out its maelstrom of conflicting sociopolitical currents: capitalism, cronyism, communism, and crime. China saw the chaos as an opportunity to realize its global ambitions, attempted to intervene, and found itself mired in regional and tribal wars and even campaigns of genocide, old hatreds given new life by the struggle to survive. Ultimately, the PRC spent billions—right before their own very different demographic problems crushed them: the number of dependent-aged persons rose to make up seventy percent of the population. The Party's solutions were logical, ruthless, and led to large scale "disaffection."

Meanwhile, the smaller but stable nations of the Developed World responded the only way they could: duck and hunker down, particularly those who had large and unstable neighbors.

And so, the globe did not plunge into complete darkness, but rather, along the predictable fault lines of developed infrastructure and geographical separation. Countries with functional economies and at great remove from the disintegrating states of South America, Asia, and particularly Africa, watched—first in horror, then in mute numbness—as almost a third of the globe's population sank into disarray, despair, and a desperate struggle for survival. And as if making good on apocalyptic prophesy, famine and death were quickly joined by war and pestilence, which only led to a greater hardening of borders.

Franklin had referred to the entire period as the Megadeath, which sounded like the name of a thrash metal band to Murphy. But it turned out that the name was not inspired by a dark poetic response to the unfolding tragedy, but by actuarial statistics. Specifically that, during the peak years of the crisis, the daily fatalities exceeded the normal average value by one million. Or about a third of a billion every year.

Ultimately, the Megadeath burned itself out. Nations restructured, began to rebuild, but the world was never quite the same. The greater powers lived with the inchoate but lingering guilt of not having done more, and the new nations nursed the grim conviction that they had been abandoned in their hour of need. Neither was completely true, yet neither was completely groundless, either.

As rebuilding began reenergizing economies and nations, cybernetic implants moved out of the realm of enhancements for the wealthy into main market. But numerous waves of hacking and targeted EMP attacks resulted in widespread avoidance. And just as that panic was dying out, the resurgent space programs of various countries collectively discovered and confirmed an object heading straight for Earth. They dubbed the interloper from the Kuiper Belt the Doomsday Rock, which was intercepted and diverted just in time to save Earth from being blasted back to the Bronze Age. Or worse.

It was, however, a galvanizing moment. Space research budgets mounted, and as access to space became habitation in space and ultimately communities in space, the competition between nations increasingly moved off Earth. One or two small wars flared and were quelled, and just after the turn of the 22nd century, a successful interstellar field effect system—the Wasserman Drive—was invented. Colonization of green worlds—a surprising, even suspicious, number of them—commenced with unusual drive and fervor.

But that lasted for just a little over a decade—because that was the point at which ruins were discovered on Delta Pavonis Three, only seven years ago. The events that followed were difficult for Murphy to keep straight: Earth tried to form a confederation; exosapients contacted humanity; what should have been a friendly meeting went sour; Earth was invaded; but with some ill-defined assistance, it threw back the occupiers and turned the tables on them in their own systems.

And just after all that was finally winding down, a mission was sent to one of those enemy's worlds: Turkh'saar. There were humans there, which should have been impossible. But there they were, anyhow—and all of them from the twentieth century. The abductees of which Franklin spoke. The so-called Lost Soldiers. Of which he was one.

And therefore, so was Murphy.

He hung his head. "I'm going to need a little time to…to take it all in."

Franklin rose. "Sure." On the seat of the other chair, he left behind what looked like a pane of glass acting like a computer screen. "We've patched the OS so that it will be easy for you to use. Anything you want to know, it'll be right there." He started toward the bulkhead door, turned back. "Need anything else?"

"Yeah." Murphy tried to grin, knew it must look feeble. "A time machine to go back home."

Franklin sighed. "You and me both, Major. You and me both." He left.

Murphy let out a long shuddering sigh and lay back on the gurney/bed. He was tired—exhausted, all of a sudden—but he didn't want to go to sleep.

Because if he did, he'd have to wake up and realize—all over again—that this was not a nightmare; it was his new reality.

* * * * *

Chapter Three
Murphy Agonistes

Waking up wasn't as bad as Murphy had anticipated, probably because he had kept at the dataslate for almost fourteen straight hours, hammering away at the history he'd missed, the technology that had arisen. He had drilled the new reality so deep and hard into his consciousness that awakening to it was not accompanied by a shock, but a deep and gnawing sense of just how much more he had to catch up on.

So, when Mssrs. Nephew and Nuncle dropped in after breakfast, he was washed, fed, and marginally informed. And had enough of his wits about him to stand and ask, "Sirs, as I understand it, at least one of you is in the U.S. armed forces, and I'm guessing that both of you rank me." He started to raise his hand into a salute.

Mr. Nuncle waved it down. "We're a little less strict about that, now, Major."

"Regulations have become more, er, casual, sir?"

"Not intentionally. However, when you are in space, you quite frequently need your hands to steady yourself. So, the protocol for salutes changed. We'll send some guidelines, if you are interested."

"I am, sirs. I was also wondering if I could perhaps call you by your real names?"

Nuncle found the same seat he'd occupied the prior day. "I would like that, Major, but I'm afraid that would not be wise. Not for us, and not for you. Please, sit down."

Murphy complied.

"You are correct that we outrank you, but that is all we are going to say on the matter. Indeed, the limited amount of information we can convey will surely be a frustration to us both."

Murphy nodded. "I suspected that. Sir. When I tried to find information on the abductees—the Lost Soldiers—I ran into a solid wall of 'access denied.' In the rare event that I was able to open a file, the material that remained was barely equal to the amount that was redacted."

Mr. Nephew smiled crookedly. "That sounds about right." His smile fell away. "We're here to give you what information we can and also to answer the questions we're allowed to."

"Very well. May I start?"

"By all means."

"*Who* won't allow you to answer all my questions?"

Nephew grinned. "That would be us. Our circumstances and official status are, well, ambiguous."

"You mean, you're renegades?"

Nuncle scratched his head. "To be perfectly frank, we're not really sure. For a number of reasons, we had to strike out on our own before we could make a full report. On several crucial matters."

"Sounds like you were one step ahead of the headsman," Murphy said with a grin.

"Could have gotten the axe," Nuncle agreed. "Or could have gotten a medal. Or both. But probably in that unfortunate order. And since we are all quite fond of keeping our heads attached to our bodies, we decided that it would be prudent to show high personal initiative and undertake our current rescue operations."

"Wait. You're trying to rescue someone, even though you're on the run?"

"Yes, that is correct. And unfortunately, that is all we may tell you."

"Why?"

Nephew leaned forward, hands clasped. "Because if the enemy gets hold of you, you can't reveal what you don't know."

Murphy hoped he didn't grow as suddenly pale as he felt he might. "Understood, sir. SOP. But, assuming the enemy are these Ktor, why would they care what I know?"

"The Ktor, or their proxies, would be very interested just to learn that there are humans from Earth running around in their space."

Murphy swallowed. "We're in their space? Right now?"

Nuncle nodded. "Have been for some weeks. And we wouldn't be here at all if there was any other way to effect the rescue. But now we have reached a crossroads, so to speak."

Murphy just nodded.

Nuncle looked uncomfortable. "I cannot divulge the size of our unit, nor its full complement. However, suffice it to say that our carrying capacity—both in terms of lading and consumables—is heavily overtaxed. That is why we had to stop in this system: 55 Tauri. We detected signs of habitation and had no choice but to risk contact. We needed to refuel and take on comestibles."

Murphy glance at Nephew. "But he said we're in enemy space."

Nephew sighed and leaned back. "I did. We are. But the Ktorans are not unified. Hell, we didn't realize just how ununified they are until we started moving through what they call the Scatters: where we are now."

"The Scatters?" Murphy echoed.

"Yeah. A stretch of space they haven't bothered to colonize. Or, to put it another way, that they decided was off limits because the competition it would have sparked among the older planets—or

'Houses'—would probably have turned into a civilization-wrecking free-for-all. So out here, it's just the descendants of their exiles."

"They have so many exiles that they leave a whole, uh, interstellar outback for them to flee to?"

Nuncle nodded. "Sounds mad, doesn't it? But that is the situation. The great powers of the Sphere have wars that escalate to the point where they are likely to get completely out of hand: nukes and planetary bombardments and the like. So, they have what you might call a pressure release valve. Any power that knows it will lose, and therefore has no reason *not* to employ maximum destructive force, is offered a choice: be exterminated or be exiled. Those who choose the latter—the Exodates—are allowed to flee into the Scatters, where they are ostensibly free to develop how and where they will, with two provisos: no FTL drives and no long-range radio comms."

"And if they ignore those restrictions?"

"Then the Sphere allows the equivalent of young-Turk bounty hunters to visit retribution upon the violators. We have seen such planets, or rather, what is left of them." Nuncle seemed to grow a little more pale than he usually was. "Not a pretty sight. And barely habitable."

"And the person or persons you're rescuing, they're someplace in these, uh—these Scatters?"

Nephew shrugged. "Might be. Might be further. That's one of the reasons we have to travel lighter. Getting there faster means a better chance of getting there in time."

Murphy looked from one to the other. "Why do I get the feeling that the conversation is moving around to the part that concerns me? Personally."

Nuncle managed to smile and be crestfallen at the same time. "And that is just the kind of insight we knew you'd have, and why you are just the man for the mission that has to be undertaken."

Oh, shit. "I see."

It was as if they had both heard his silent *"Oh, shit."* "Yes," Nuncle said with a nod. "I'm afraid you are about to get the dirty end of the stick, Major. Here's the situation:

"We can't abandon much of our equipment. We are too likely to need it for either fighting through to the rescue point or once we get there. The only thing we have too much of is, well, bodies in cold sleep. They take up space, draw power, and if we find ourselves in a situation where we needed to reanimate all of them, we'd be out of food within days.

"We discovered that there are friendly communities in this companion system, all of whom live in space, on concealed habitats. They go into hiding whenever the malign forces from the main system put in their occasional but largely predictable appearance. We, however, were not aware of that when we intercepted their very subtle communications and announced ourselves."

Murphy grimaced. "Let me guess: by announcing yourselves to them, you also announced yourself to the malign forces from the main system."

Nephew nodded. "Yep. We blew their centuries-old cover in a single afternoon. So, we had to make it right. Which meant locating and taking out all the spaceside opposition and any ground-based communication sites the OpFor had for sending word back to the main system."

Murphy stared at him. "But that means their HQ back home has got to be realizing that its task force to this system has gone off the grid. Entirely. They're gonna want to know what happened, and how."

Nuncle nodded vigorously. "Precisely. And that is where you—and others—come in."

Why am I not surprised? "Sir, I don't mean to be uncooperative, but I'm not part of your formation."

Nephew's expression was like he was pulling a long splinter out of his foot. "Actually, Major, you are. This came up when the awakened Lost Soldiers were exfilled from Turkh'saar. Technically, the missing were never mustered out of their different services. Besides, beyond fixing the problem we caused for the friendlies here in 55 Tauri B, there's also this: we can't take all of the Lost Soldiers with us. Not anymore. We've run the logistics. In fact, you know the person who cranked those numbers. Missy Katano."

Murphy started. "From Mogadishu? Yes, I knew her. Well, I knew *of* her. She was the grease that made the wheels turn in logistics. She was on the chopper. So, she made it?"

"As we told you, only the crew chief and the copilot were lost. The rest of you were—salvaged—by the Ktor. And don't ask me how. Not all their methods are a mystery, but in your case and a few others, we have no idea how they got people out of sinking wrecks before they drowned." He shook his head. "Anyhow, we have to leave almost one hundred of the Lost Soldiers behind, along with their gear and a small number of vehicles. Just enough for you to fulfill your first objectives."

The operational nitty gritty was shit to hear, too, but at least this kind of shit was familiar to Murphy: new superiors setting impossible objectives. "And what is that first objective, sirs?"

"Objective*s*, Major Murphy," Nuncle stressed. "They must be pursued concurrently. Firstly, once you are landed on this system's habitable planet, you must commandeer indigenous equipment. This is both because there is no certainty of resupply and because there must be a minimal Terran—er, Earth-force footprint. The only way to do that is to blend in with the locals: use their equipment, learn their languages, adopt their ways. Where practicable and ethical."

"And the other objective? Sir?"

Nephew was sitting ramrod straight in his chair now. "As we said, we eliminated all the spaceside comm platforms that could reach back to the main system. And we took out the ground installations that we knew of which had a similar capability. But the OpFor still has units on the ground. Creating a long-range transmitter isn't rocket science. It isn't easy, but we can be sure that some of the OpFor knows how to do it and is taking the necessary steps."

Murphy rubbed the bridge of his nose. "And I'm supposed to locate and eliminate them with less than a hundred men, sirs?"

Nuncle shook his head. "The spaceside locals have means of introducing you favorably to R'Bak's locals, the ones that the opposition forces raid and then 'cull' when they arrive. You won't lack allies."

Well, it was nice that at least *one* bit of good news had popped up. "Sirs, I'd like to go back a moment. You mentioned that there is 'no certainty of resupply.' Could you expand upon that, please?"

Nuncle looked at Nephew, who sighed and rested his hands on his knees. "Major, it is our intent to come back this way. We're confident that you will succeed in your further objectives: to establish a secure operating base for yourselves and for us to retire to for resupply, should our rescue efforts prove to require multiple journeys beyond the Scatters.

"Unfortunately, it is just as possible that we will not return. That we will run into the Ktor. Or their proxies. Or any one of a thousand different anomalies that are a death sentence when you are operating in uncharted space. So, yes, unfortunately, there is no guarantee of resupply. But I promise you this: we mean to come back and either evacuate you or reinforce your position."

"If any of us are still here and breathing," Murphy added.

Nephew just nodded. "That's the op, Major."

Murphy didn't feel like he might puke, but he certainly wanted to spit in disgust. "I understand, sir. Sounds like I have a lot to accomplish."

Nuncle got that hangdog look that always seemed to precede some dire addition from him. "You do indeed, Major. And I'm afraid there's one further challenge of which you must be apprised."

Of course there is. "Yes, sir?"

"Your men for this mission—the Lost Soldiers we've chosen—are not necessarily the most coherent force."

Great. "I'm not sure I understand what you mean by that, sir."

"Major, our rescue mission will be almost constantly in space. When traveling in that unforgiving environment, you need individuals who are self-starters, not easily distracted from their task, team players. In short, in space or new exoplanetary environments, there are often crises that arise quickly and without warning. The soldiers best able to survive are the ones who are most dedicated to their profession, to their job."

Better still. "Sir, does this mean I'm getting a bunch of...of discipline cases?"

"Not entirely, Major. Some have demonstrated phobias that would paralyze them in space—claustrophobia and agoraphobia are two such, despite being direct opposites. There are individuals who do not handle contact with alien life forms well. There are others who have expressed religious difficulties operating alongside intelligent beings that are not human. And yes, you are also drawing the con-artists, black marketeers, and barracks lawyers."

Total perfection. "Sounds like I'll have to whip them into shape before they'll be ready for duty. Sirs."

Nephew nodded. "True, but you won't have to do it alone. The other survivors from the crash are going to be your cadre, minus Missy and Dr. Hampson. That gives you a number of excellent officers who are, variously, specialists who can oversee air, space, armor, even ground and spec ops."

It was a pretty narrow ray of hope—but a ray, nonetheless. "Any reason why all of us crash survivors are being selected?"

"Three reasons, Major. First, since all of you were taken during one of the last abductions, you have the best understanding of truly modern warfare. You're going to need that. Secondly, once again, being from the late 20th century, the abductors were able to get data on all of you, mostly from the civilian sector. Consequently, if we took you on the rescue mission and ran into the Ktor, any of you who were captured or unrecoverable could possibly be ID'd by them. And then the Ktor would have all the grounds they need for declaring war. Hell, they'd almost have to, given their own cultural standards and expectations. And third, all of you are among the very best at what you do."

"No insolence intended, sir, but how the heck do you know that?"

Nephew smiled. "Like I said, the late-stage abductors were able to get various records pertaining to the people they grabbed. And with help from the exosapients you'd call 'grays,' we were finally able to access and decode the records on the Lost Soldiers. At least, those whose cryocells we still possess." He leaned back. "We may be giving you a challenging bunch of troops, Major, but you are going to have an outstanding cadre with which to whip them into shape and get the job done."

Murphy discovered that his eyes were drifting to the floor. He didn't want to say anything else, but he had to. They had to know. "Sirs, I am not sure my records were updated by the Ktor in time to reflect this, but...I was diagnosed with MS right before the chopper went down. Not quite twenty-four hours earlier. That's the reason I was being shipped stateside, to confirm the diagnosis and take me off the line. So my condition could not endanger others."

Nuncle nodded soberly. "Yes, Major Murphy. We know. We also know that we do not exist in a perfect world. Neither you in terms of your personal health, nor us in terms of our operational imperatives. Under any other circumstances, we would have kept you in stasis until and unless we could access a cure.

"But you may be interested to learn that the Blackhawk's pilot, whom we awoke before you, conducted joint operations with the locals against the OpFor. She gained their trust, made several friends among them. Through a few carefully tailored and coached questions, she was able to determine that neither the spaceside nor dirtside locals have any record of MS or its symptoms among their population. And those records go back almost two millennia.

"This is particularly interesting in light of the fact that the habitable planet in this companion system—R'Bak—is an object of contention precisely because it is a source of various flora with powerful and highly unusual therapeutic properties."

"And you think one of those plants is going to prove to be a miracle cure for MS? That's a pretty long shot, don't you think, sir?"

Nuncle nodded sadly. "I agree. On the other hand, it is, as you Yanks say, the only shot you've got. But that's the compassionate side of the equation of putting you in charge. The practical side is that you are very early in the course of the disease and have an outstanding record, along with outstanding recommendations from your superiors and your subordinates, right down to scuttlebutt from E1s and E2s." He stood, Nephew following a moment later.

Murphy rose also. "One last thing, sirs. I understand what our mission is. But I don't know why we are doing it, what's at stake."

"That is part of what we need to keep close, Major."

Murphy cleared his throat. "Permission to speak freely, sirs."

Both nodded.

"Listen, if you expect me to get people to keep fighting toward an objective, light years from a home they may never see again, I have to be able to tell them *something*. I have to be able to tell them why it matters. Otherwise, they are going to walk away thinking that you're just ditching them to lighten your load. That they are just garbage you're off-loading and that you're just shining us on with a bullshit mission, a fiction meant to convince us that we're not just being left here to die. Which won't work, sirs."

Nephew and Nuncle looked at each other. Nephew squared his shoulders as he turned toward Murphy again. "Okay. Then you can tell them this. The Ktor are derived from *homo sapiens*. They can pass unnoticed amongst us. They tricked other races into invading and almost conquering Earth. They want to take us over, to make us a part of their Sphere and grab our DNA to help boost their fading, overtaxed generations." He leaned forward slightly. "And you can add this, if you want. They killed my father, gutted my sister so that she's on permanent life support, and have tried—or succeeded in—destroying almost everything else that I love. And they'll do the same to you, to all the Lost Soldiers, and every good and beautiful thing you remember on planet Earth." He leaned back and his voice became quiet again. "Is that cause enough, Major?"

Murphy swallowed. "Sir, yes, sir." Then: "Where do I start?"

* * * * *

Chapter Four
Murphy Alone

Murphy leaned back, having just jabbed a period at the end of his most recent log entry. The change in posture once again brought his eyes level with the op-center's forward observation screen. The view from Outpost's bow was mesmerizing: a slowly falling starfield on endless loop, repeating every seventy seconds.

He forced himself to look back down before the Zen-trance of the cycling image put him to sleep. Which would not have surprised anyone in the operations center. Murphy had been standing oversight on final approach and insertion for twenty hours straight, and at a certain point, stim tabs lost their efficacy.

However, just because the others in the op-center would be unsurprised did not mean they would be understanding. Rather, they were likely to see grogginess as yet another confirmation of their perception of him, and, by extension, the rest of the Lost Soldiers from Earth. Namely, that they were undisciplined, imprecise, ill-trained, dim-witted, and clumsy.

It was hard to argue the last point, at least as long as they were spaceside. Even in the long, hollow asteroids that Murphy's men now inhabited, they remained awkward, still acclimating to the .75-gee equivalent. There was also their lack of adaptation to the Coriolis effect. Specifically, their planet-trained eyes had not yet learned to predict the seemingly curved trajectories of free flying or moving objects in a rotating environment. Nor had they learned to anticipate the potential for disorientation when they turned their heads perpendicular to the direction of the spin. Accordingly, the locals—the SpinDogs, as they called themselves—were not simply fabricating an unflattering characterization when they labeled their guests "awkward"—the Terrans were broader, heavier, and stumbled around like inebriated gorillas. Among the most prejudiced locals, the Hardliners, the term "Terran" was being supplanted by "Trog." Murphy considered the odds to be about fifty percent that it would become the most common label for his people.

Unless, of course, the Lost Soldiers decisively proved their claimed superiority in a planetary environment. Which they were about to do, and which was why Murphy had been in Outpost's opcenter for the past twenty hours. Officially, he was a coordinator of the first joint Terran-SpinDog mission to the surface of R'Bak. But more essentially, he was the guardian angel for the two Lost Soldiers assigned to it. The SpinDogs were friends of a sort, but the relationship was still young and not all of them were happy with it. Not happy at all.

He checked his G-Shock; only fourteen minutes to orbital insertion. Time enough to make sure that the mission log entry he'd just completed made some kind of sense when read in the context of all the ones he'd written before. He flipped open the green-covered, ring-bound notebook he'd dragged with him all the way from Fort Benning, and started at the top:

MISSION LOG

CO: MURPHY, R. Y., MAJOR

LOCAL YEAR: 672 SR (Date coding note: SR stands for "Since Rev." Origin of "SR" uncertain. Could refer to spaceside locals' first official recording of years (i.e.; revolutions around the local star), the political revolts that compelled the SpinDogs to leave R'Bak, or the founding of their first spin habitat.)

LOCAL DATE: Day 048 (of 369) (Time sync note: Local days are only 18 hours. Consequently, the local year of 369 days is actually only 75 percent the duration of one Earth year.

EARTH DATE: August 30, 2125 AD

PreOp / Strategic SITREP (approximate):

Increasing competition among powers in the primary system (Jrar) may have prompted several nations on the main planet (Kulsis) to move up the timetable on exploitation of R'Bak during the imminent Searing. First mission arrived in this system (secondary star, Shex) 18 months earlier than on any previous Searing. ELINT and SIGINT both indicate that the OpFor is from Kulsis' second largest power, which has an entente/détente relationship with the greatest/oldest/traditionalist power.

Due to OpFor's early arrival at R'Bak, SpinDog and RockHounds (two different branches of the spaceside local population) had neither instituted full cessation of travel nor completed re-concealment of stationary assets. Many were compelled to go into hiding wherever they were, including various resource collection teams on the second planet, V'dyr, and one trade mission concluding business on R'Bak.

Day

000 Ship carrying Lost Soldiers (Dornaani hull *Olsloov*) arrives in system, scans, discovers SpinDogs on far side of local sun (Shex). Observes, decodes comms. Language is quickly identified as a devolved form of Ktor as it was spoken almost 1,400 years ago (approximation only). Despite linguistic roots, *Olsloov* command staff deems it unlikely that the SpinDogs would become aggressive or that they have had any recent contact with the Ktoran Sphere.

001 Contact made by Olsloov command staff. Purpose: acquire consumables.

002 No response, but Spin/Rock ships move to avoid further LoS/lascom messages. Pickets of harvesters/raiders notice movement of the previously undetected Spin/Rock craft, begin maneuvering at extremely high gee (often 2-3, sustained) to effect intercept. Terran cadre analyzes the situation; *Olsloov* selectively jams OpFor broad-comms. Only transmission completed by OpFor was decrypted as "Investigating local anomaly; stand by for details." Narrow-beam comms blocked by position of companion star (Shex), which occluded receivers located in the primary (Jrar) system.

003 Sensor results from *Olsloov* indicate that OpFor's hi-gee maneuvers are consistent with a) intercept of SpinDog craft and b) repositioning to clear transmission coordinates to Jrar. Capt. Mara Lee, USAF, is restored from cryogenic suspension to assist in battlefield support and liaison duty with SpinDog matriarchy.

004 Contact established with Spin/Rock leadership using Dornaani translation system to update language from classic Ktor and to

crack cyphers. Agreement reached. Compromised Spin/Rock craft adjust course to flee toward prearranged coordinates in outer system. Intercept trajectory for OpFor intersects optimal ambush point for *Olsloov* and her drones/ROVs. Captain Lee receives partial accelerated training in local language via virtuality immersion.

006 OpFor pursuit elements ambushed by *Olsloov* at edge of outer system. Tech superiority of *Olsloov* and her deployed assets results in complete elimination of enemy hulls without loss or significant damage. In and near R'Bak orbit, Dornaani ROVs (with direct oversight from Captain Lee) assist Spin/Rock assets to eliminate small number of OpFor hulls (mostly interface transports) and sensors. Dornaani standoff drones eliminate two planetside comm arrays with potential to reach Jrar system.

007 *Olsloov* arrives on-station at R'Bak, conducts close survey for further planetside comm facilities with inter-system capability. None located. AARs generated and shared by *Olsloov* and Spin/Rock cadres.

008 Data sharing and first meetings between *Olsloov* and Spin/Rock leadership. Mutual support and joint operation agreements reached. Captain Lee is debriefed by *Olsloov* cadre and resumes accelerated language training via virtuality technology.

009 Transfer of volatiles and other consumables to *Olsloov* commences. Captain Lee completes accelerated language training.

010 Data packets for tech sharing and replication of 20th century Earth weapons and systems relayed to and declared operational by Spin/Rock automated production facilities. Examples of each system are provided from legacy examples carried aboard

Olsloov. Legacy examples include helicopters, weapons, ammunition, simple electronics. Captain Lee commences training of first class of SpinDog rotary wing pilots.

013 Major RY Murphy restored from cryogenic suspension. Debrief commences.

014 Major Murphy debrief ends. Light company of Lost Soldiers detached for R'Bak ops is revived.

015 R'Bak ops contingent (Lost Soldiers) commences accelerated language training aboard *Olsloov*. *Olsloov* and seeded (permanent) microsat net detect upswing in movement by advanced vehicles on surface of R'Bak.

016 First planetside training sorties of SpinDog RWP pilots led by Captain Lee. Planetside movement increase is confirmed as OpFor activity. Spin/Rock intel assessment is that they are gathering resources to secure optimum construction site for transmitter capable of reaching Jrar system.

017 Guildmother/Matriarch of leading Spin/Rock Family reported to *Olsloov* as MIA planetside on R'Bak while conducting undisclosed SAR ops in north polar extents. Capt. Lee is cleared for, and tasked to, effect recovery of Guildmother/Matriarch, attached personnel, and others requiring rescue.

018 Capt. Lee's recovery mission achieves objective while sustaining moderate casualties, but Guildmother/Matriarch had been mortally wounded prior to her arrival in AO.

019 *Olsloov* cadre, Lost Soldier CO Murphy, and SpinDog leadership agrees to conops of joint contact and recruitment mission to R'Bak. Objective: gather sufficient indigenous forces and commandeer cached Kulsis equipment to disrupt and prevent OpFor construction of dirtside inter-system comm array. Space-

side requirements articulated; assets identified. Preps begin. Construction of improvised meteoritic assault capsules commences, with limited assistance from Dornaani and contemporary Terrans. Mission leadership selected and briefed. Training commences.

021 Lost Soldier R'Bak detachment completes language training, skills assessment, physical readiness conditioning, and is officially stood up as an active unit. Designation pending.

022 *Olsloov* completes replenishment activities, prepares for departure. Training for joint mission to R'Bak concludes. Objectives and targets updated. Final briefing.

023 *Olsloov* departs.

024 Mission dropship commences op with tug boost toward R'Bak along retrograde orbital track.

028 Dropship lascom confirms all parameters are nominal; mission on track.

Murphy read his last entry. In minutes, he would know what fateful emendation he would have to make to that final clause: "mission on track."

But the actions that would determine the change he would have to make were out of his hands, as they were for everyone else in Outpost. That would be decided in real time by the crew of the dropship and the joint ops team, now almost thirty million kilometers behind them.

"Behind" them? Murphy frowned at himself: in space, nothing was ever really "behind" or "in front" of you, any more than the terms up and down had any real utility. But it was hard getting used to the strange terms that prevailed when trying to establish spatial relation-

ships independent of gravity or fixed objects. Still, no better time than the present...

So: "behind." Murphy pinched the bridge of his nose, tried to visualize the actual positions of the objects in question. Outpost shared R'Bak's orbit around Shex. However, it preceded R'Bak in that orbital track, maintaining a constant distance of a bit over 22 million kilometers—which was also .15 AU (astral units). Or, more significantly, 75 light-seconds. And because it was "ahead" of R'Bak in the same orbit (anything up to 180 degrees in the lead was deemed "ahead"), Outpost was "spinward" of the planet. Conversely, any object following up to 180 degrees "behind" R'Bak was deemed to be "trailing" it.

So, in the shorthand of everyone from the 22nd century—aliens included—R'Bak and the dropship carrying the ops team were presently .15 AU to the "trailing" of Outpost. Murphy pinched the bridge of his nose again. When he had enough time to write the terms down or think them through, they all made sense. But then the locals started rattling them off in their high-speed jabber, often adding two positional coordinates that could either be oriented to the system's ecliptic *or* to the observer's own location and attitude. That was when Rodger Y. Murphy conceded defeat and simply resolved to wear an expression of calm focus instead of slack-jawed confusion.

Which was pretty much the same expression he had worn the first time he saw Outpost from the bridge of the spindly RockHound "packet" that brought him out from the largest of the habitats: Spin One.

Like the "spins," Outpost was an oblong asteroid. But whereas the spins revolved around their long axes, like huge stony logs rolling slowly in place, Outpost was tumbling ass-over-eyeballs. So, where the spins' centripetally-generated "gees" held your feet down upon their long inner walls, at Outpost, the maximum gees were felt at its ends. Murphy had come to envision it as living and working inside the rubber caps of a high-school twirler's baton, the soles of his feet racing past the faces in the watching crowd.

Shortly after arriving, he'd made the mistake of commenting that these features made Outpost seem like a pretty awkward choice for a facility so proximal to R'Bak. When the ops support staff from the Hardliner families had drifted away hiding (but not really) sneers of contempt, a comparatively tolerant Expansionist technician had explained that Major Murphy could not be more mistaken in his assessment.

Firstly, Outpost was the closest semi-stable object from which they could watch R'Bak. Murphy accepted this as proof that the mantra of 20th century real-estate agents was universal: location, location, location! Specifically, Outpost had started its existence as part of the swarm of planetoids that any planet captured in both the spinward and trailing equilibrium points of its orbit. Murphy had actually heard of those, they were called LaGrangian points. Unfortunately, that infobite did not impress the technician in the slightest. In retrospect, Murphy supposed trying to impress her with his space knowledge was the equivalent of her proudly pointing out how, when trees grow close together in a big bunch, that's called a *forest*!

However, Outpost was, in every way, an outlier from the asteroids in R'Bak's spinward LaGrangian—or Trojan—point. Not only had it fallen thirty million kilometers behind that cluster, but its end-over end tumble was both uncommon and unusually "clean." By which she meant that its motion was all along the vector Murphy thought of as pitch; there was almost none of what he called roll or yaw. The terms the locals' used to describe these vectors of motion made no sense to him and did not seem to have transliterations; they were not inherited from the cant of mariners, and the technician gave no clue as to their origins.

Considered together, she concluded, this made Outpost an extremely fortuitous find for the SpinDogs. Murphy frowned, expressed concern that the rock's unusual tumble might attract unwanted attention.

The technician's lips strained into an indulgent smile. Even if the spacefaring monsters from the Jrar system began to suspect the existence of space-dwellers somewhere among the planets and asteroids of Shex, a freakish rock like Outpost would be the *last* place they'd check. Just over 800 meters long, and with a spin rate that provided barely sufficient gee-forces to a small portion of its opposed poles, it could not support a viable long-duration community. Consequently, the raiders' first searches would be for something more like the spins themselves: long, large asteroids in slow, stable rolls. But the only reason the invaders from Kulsis would ever search at all was if they detected movement, artifacts, or emissions that did not originate with them. Which was why the present mission to R'Bak had been launched in the first place: to ensure that the Spin-Dogs and RockHounds remained undiscovered and unsuspected.

One of the more Hardline overseers—the ops command group had been carefully drawn from across the SpinDogs' and RockHounds' strange political spectrum—glanced sharply in Murphy's direction but did not make eye contact. "Drop time is on track: two minutes."

Murphy resisted the impulse to chew on his lip or cuticle or both. "Two minutes" actually meant "forty-five seconds until their capsules are released and then seventy-five seconds for word to reach us." Meaning that in just a little over half a minute now, the first part of this insanely ambitious—not to say risky—plan would begin. And by the time that word reached him, the outcome would already belong not to the present, but to history. As would the ops team if things went wrong.

And me, too, maybe. Murphy reached for his water bulb in the low gravity, affected a bored, roving stare as he sipped. But behind his (hopefully) duty-dulled eyes, he assessed the faces in the ops center. *Which of them might have orders to cut their Family's losses if the insertion fails?* It was no secret that many of the leading Families among the SpinDogs had felt it better to go to ground—hide hard and deep—rather than try to go planetside in an attempt to silence the remaining interlopers from the Jrar system.

There were a lot of flaws with their "hide and do nothing" strategy, of course. If the thugs, failed rent-a-cops, and contractor wannabes now on R'Bak made like E.T. and phoned home, there'd be little to zero chance of the SpinDogs and RockHounds remaining undetected. But if one or more Families had a contingency for that, had maybe decided to sell out the others in order to become spaceside satraps who swore service to the overlords on Kulsis, well, in that case…

Murphy finished scanning the room as he returned the water bulb to its holder. He wasn't sure what signs of incipient treachery he'd hoped to detect. None of them wore facial hair, so any unrevealed villains among them didn't have greasy mustachios to twirl. Still, it stood to reason that if one or more Families had a contingency plan for mission failure, it probably involved either a cover-up or selling out directly to the Kulsians. Either way, that put every Terran in the system at risk, Dornaani promises of return and reward—or retribution—notwithstanding. For the SpinDogs and RockHounds, alien promises and threats were a distant maybe; a visit from the bloodthirsty and ruthless Kulsians was an already-established, in-your-face fact.

But how could he be sure if such contingency plans even existed? Or if there was only *one* such plan? Or which of the faces in the ops center would be the expediters? *Hell, I'm an infantry officer, not James-friggin-Bond. I can't tell who they are—*

But… but maybe I don't have to.

Murphy stood into the one-third gee, looked at his watch for theatrical purposes. "In the event that the mission is a failure, I will need your collective cooperation on comms."

The most stone-hearted Hardliner didn't keep all the contempt out of his voice. "You mean, to inform the rest of your men of their comrades' tragic sacrifice in a timely fashion?"

"No, in order to ensure that the Dornaani microsat net does not self-destruct."

All around the ops center, hooded eyes opened wide. An overseer from one of the Expansionist Families stood. "What do you mean?"

Murphy checked his watch again. "There is little time to explain. Briefly: in addition to me, my cadre were all given failsafe implants. If we die, the implant ceases to signal. When it stops, the net self-destructs."

"We have detected no such signals during—"

Murphy rode over the top of that and other nascent objections. "Since the signal frequency and interval are not known to anyone—even us—but are preprogrammed into the Dornaani satellites and control elements, there is no way to know if we would have seconds or days before the next failsafe check. In order to maintain the tactical advantages"—*to put it lightly*—"conferred by the microsat network, I will need to act with all haste. Please stand ready to re-task your lascom links to the coordinates I shall provide. If it becomes necessary."

Murphy sat. The ops center was silent for a long moment, and then a distempered buzz of murmurs and whispers rose up. He could guess the content: that the Terran major was lying; that he was *not* lying; that he was bluffing; that this duplicity was expected; that it was wholly unanticipated; that even Dornaani technology was not capable of sustaining such a subtle failsafe system over such extraordinary distances; that if the microsat net were lost, the SpinDogs and RockHounds would be blind to events on R'Bak just when they needed to see them more than ever.

But Murphy didn't care which they believed, because at the base of it all, they would realize that any contingency plans to disappear the rest of the Lost Soldiers or present them as a bloody gift to the captains of Kulsis, now had to be paused. For a few days, at the very least. Maybe permanently. And that would give Murphy time enough to pull another plan or ploy out of his ass.

He hoped.

It wasn't pure fabrication; the Dornaani *had* rigged their microsats with a failsafe. It just wasn't arranged along the lines that Murphy had drawn for his suddenly sullen and mistrustful audience.

The now fury-faced Hardliner looked up again. "Signal received from the dropship; capsules have been deployed. Now entering upper atmosphere. Telemetry and instrumentation nominal."

Murphy held in a sigh of relief, thought it might burst out of his gut or lungs. So, in order to maintain an expression of calm, almost bored composure, he reached out for the logbook and scanned down for his last entry:

028 Dropship confirmed all parameters are nominal; mission on track.

He erased the concluding words, and wrote instead:

028 Dropship confirmed all parameters are nominal; orbital insertion confirmed.

He leaned back again, fought against the downward drag of his suddenly heavy eyelids, and wondered how long it would be before the op team would be able to make contact.

If they survive the drop, that is.

* * * * *

Book One
Shakes

By Mike Massa

Chapter One

Damn. I've heard of getting the shakes during a drop, but this is ridiculous.

The insertion capsule was shuddering violently as it slowed, plunging deeper into the gravity well of the new planet. Despite all the precautions, both his limited equipment and body were rattling uncomfortably against the improvised padding and alloy bracing, creating a rapid thrumming. The little cone-shaped ship had stubby wings, but the thin atmosphere at high altitude denied them purchase. Dynamic forces snapped the vehicle back and forth across several degrees of pitch and yaw every second, resembling a ride inside the paint mixer of his father's hardware store. The very worst of the uncomfortable oscillations made his vision gray out. Harry tried to relax, deliberately inhaling through his mouth and exhaling through his nose, as the rapid vibration created an ever louder metallic banging which was growing alarming. He had no idea if this was normal or not.

It was his first space drop.

Lieutenant Harold Tapper, formerly of the United States Navy, fought to clear his vision as he scanned the scant handful of monochromatic screens facing his acceleration cradle. A red peanut light began to blink as the adjacent display flashed a block of alternating black and gray text. The accompanying warning siren was mostly drowned out by the hammering sounds made by the tortured hull of the ship. His blurring eyesight made the mostly incomprehensible alien script useless, not that it would have made any difference during the meteoric insertion via a scratch-built pod. Regardless, he was pretty sure the alarm wasn't a good sign.

Unfortunately for Harry, his automated single person craft was lean on comfort and instruments, sharing those qualities with his last ride on the UH-60 Blackhawk which had ferried him out of Mogadishu almost one hundred and fifty years ago. Of course, that helicopter had been built in a proper factory. This *thing* had exposed fasteners and there were parts simply *glued* together. On the other hand, there wasn't a window from which to see his surroundings. If he wanted a better view, he'd have to wait until this sorry excuse for a spaceship came apart around him. Which was, come to think of it, the last thing he remembered from that Blackhawk ride.

An especially severe bit of turbulence rattled his teeth together for a moment. Some things never changed. He was still a passenger, entirely at the mercy of a product from the lowest bidder and the whim of the gods.

Harry felt a change as the automated systems won out against the high-altitude winds, orienting his craft on the drop zone far below. Abruptly, the ride calmed. Even better, Harry's earpiece pinged an alert as the networked systems aboard the other two aeroshells automatically re-established contact.

"Seeker Six, this is Five," Rodriguez said, reporting in. Sergeant First Class Marco Rodriguez was the only other Terran on this trip. "Hey, boss, everything okay over there? This ride is fucking number ten, like a Saigon boom-boom gi—"

"Five, this is Six," Harry replied, stepping on the Green Beret's transmission, using their new shared language instead of his mother tongue. "No English. Ktoran only. I'm good. How about you, over?"

"Well, there ain't no red lights flashing anymore," Rodriguez replied, using the language they shared with the third member of their team. "Now all I need is to wake up from this dream and find myself in the land of the Big PX."

"Copy that, Marco. Break, Four, this is Six, come in."

"I hear you, Lieutenant," an accented tenor voice answered him in perfect English, no doubt making a point to the primitives from Earth. Volo Zobulakos' English was better than Harry's High Ktor, despite the forced learning program many of the Terrans had endured during their brief time awake on the Dornaani cruiser. He continued in the clipped syllables of his own language. "Passing thirty-five thousand meters. All systems nominal. Tracking directly for the principal LZ. Parachute deployment in two hundred and twenty seconds."

Harry acknowledged the transmission and ran through his sparsely populated landing checklist. Despite having nothing to do but wait for nearly four minutes, Harry compulsively scanned the inside of his capsule for the hundredth time. The stealthy re-entry vehicles were the product of the spacefaring civilization to which Volo belonged. In fact, his entire people, nicknamed the SpinDogs, were now entirely based off-planet and had been for hundreds of years. Technologically, they were far, far ahead of the re-usable space shuttles which had been the state of art in America when Harry had deployed to Operation RESTORE HOPE in Somalia. However, this disposable and stealthy one-man capsule wasn't the way he'd expected to be inserted. Harry had seen myriad craft in use around the SpinDogs' habitats. From the single person scooters used to prospect in the asteroid clusters to large intra-system shuttlecraft, the SpinDogs had plenty of options for delivering the little team. However, the small, space-based civilization was paranoid to the point of making the average Explosive Ordinance Demolition tech seem careless.

Rather than risk the detection and possible destruction of the dropship *Hidden Knife*, they'd eschewed a landing and chosen the simpler option of dropping individual personnel capsules in the vicinity of the target. If the mission succeeded, they could recover and recycle the aeroshells at leisure. If the mission failed, the SpinDogs were out three unpowered craft, two Lost Soldiers, and one very expendable scion of an upstart House.

Harry expected that the Terrans didn't count, of course.

He watched the shiny digital altimeter count down as they fell toward the surface, just like a normal parachute jump. Instead of the old-school HALO method all SEALs practiced, back when there had been SEALs, this was something Major Murphy had dubbed an "OILO," or Orbital Insertion Low Opening operation. It seemed unlikely any of the Kulsian raiders which had survived the strike against their orbital assets and planetary comm would be maintaining a radar net, but the clandestine drop also reduced the likelihood of visual detection. Much like the spec ops mission profiles back on Earth, Harry's little team would survive by using discretion and craft, not brute firepower.

That was a good thing because his current mission wasn't even half-baked. Harry still wasn't convinced this was the best Earth's supposed allies and keepers of some high and mighty interstellar compact, the Dornaani, could do. Dump six dozen archaic humans on an enemy-occupied planet in order to secure a fallback point for a larger-scale mission which was itself just shy of being a forlorn hope? Entrust opening negotiations to an unproven local and a pair of junior military personnel? Convince your new allies to risk everything for strangers? And yet, here he was, hurtling downward like so much cargo.

Harry looked intently at one of the few manual controls in the vehicle. The big red lever located between his knees was labeled in blocky Ktor script, but next to it some helpful wag among his English-speaking comrades had taped a label, "Manual Deployment. Not For Use Underwater. Activate Only In Atmosphere!" The next panel over included an electronic warfare warning menu which would warn of potentially hostile radar. Mercifully, it remained blank. That suggested the close approach of the drop ship had gone unnoticed.

Something was going right, anyway. So much for Murphy's Law.

At which point a second red light began to blink as the previously blank EW alert flashed. The capsule abruptly turned, loading so many gees on Harry he didn't have time to register surprise, let alone make a last radio call, before blacking out.

He came to an unknown time later, but the ride was back to being smooth. The radio comms weren't.

"—ome in! Seeker Six, come in!"

"This is Six. What the hell, over?" Harry replied muzzily.

"Parachute deployment in thirty seconds!" Volo said urgently.

Harry shook his head and yawned, then looked at the instruments. Crap, they were very nearly on the surface! There was no time to be surprised; he needed to work the problem. The shortness of the landing checklist didn't make his situation any less dire.

"Ten seconds!" Volo said, unnecessarily warning both Terrans.

"Prepare for manual deployment."

If Marco Rodriguez was anything like Harry, he was watching the altimeter with growing apprehension. An impatient SpinDog technician had carefully repeated the instructions to an audience he doubtless regarded as incapable of using tools more sophisticated than rocks and sharp sticks. In theory, each craft would use a flicker laser to sense the minimum height-over-ground required for deployment of the chute to guarantee a safe landing. If he didn't feel the automated systems deploy the capsule's drogue and parachute combination, he'd have less than two seconds to mechanically initiate that critical step. Harry placed both hands on the pebbly surface of the L-shaped lever and took a deep breath. He watched his displays intently, counting down internally.

In three, two, o—

He was interrupted by the audible *pop* of the drogue ribbon launching over his head. One of his screens flashed the corresponding message, as the drogue gave his capsule a single, hard jerk, pressing him heavily into his couch. After dramatically slowing the freefall to a speed the twin parachutes could withstand, the drogue detached. A second, mushier jerk announced the canopies' successful opening.

The capsule had barely steadied underneath the green and brown parachutes before the capsule crashed to a painful stop. The scant padding on the seat might have prevented any serious injury, but Harry still ached all over. But like the pain caused by a misaligned crotch strap during a regular jump, this was a good sort of pain to have. The parachute had worked, and the capsule was down. The cone-shaped vehicle came to rest on its side, however. Getting out was going to require a bit of scrambling.

"Four, Five, this is Six," he said, trusting the hands-free microphone on his helmet while hanging sideways in his straps. "Sound off."

"Five on the ground. Mind the first step, it's a doozy," Rodriguez said jauntily.

"I've opened the hatch already, Lieutenant," Volo answered. "It's daylight, and we must cover the ships immediately."

"Copy," Harry said, releasing his chest strap. He fell heavily against one of the instrument panels, painfully bruising his arm. He suppressed a heartfelt curse.

"Popping the hatch."

He reached for the door lever, now inconveniently located over his head. After a pause, the capsule verified his intent, requiring a second yank before it obediently ejected the hatch outward with a percussive *bang*. Instantly, a cold wind filled his capsule, making him shiver. He poked his head outside and surveyed a bleak and rocky landscape which was partially obscured by the capsule's billowing parachute.

After donning a hooded parka from a storage cabinet underneath his feet, he withdrew his personal equipment and weapon. Then, with an athleticism he didn't feel, Harry used an inner handhold to swing outside. On either side of his aeroshell, the terrain rose several meters in elevation, forming a shallow canyon. His 'chute was tangled in some stunted gray-green trees that bordered the drop zone. Knee high, rust-colored spiky grass poked up in between the fist-sized stones covering much of the ground. The breeze smelled wet and musty, but the ground appeared dry. A football field distant, Harry could make out another capsule, and began trotting over. It was supposed to be dusk on R'Bak, but the overcast diffused the light. Out of reflex, he checked his wristwatch, which rode alongside a new gadget doubling as a short-range radio and compass. Both were still set to SpinDog station time, adopted during the mission prep. He supposed he could check with Volo. It didn't matter yet. Experience had taught the SEAL exactly what time it was.

The local hour is half past "your ass is in a sling." My team is untested and outnumbered, the local population is mostly hostile, the wildlife carnivorous, and, in two years, the local star is going to approach its binary twin, boiling the oceans and scorching the land. Oh, and your extract off-planet depends entirely on mission success, so don't screw up.

Welcome to R'Bak.

* * * * *

Chapter Two

Harry couldn't even hear the noise of the Mog, anymore. Just Sara's voice and stateside sounds low in the background. He tried to get his ear closer to the phone without being aware of it in his hand.

I'm sorry for everything. I'm sorry I was such an asshole.

I'm sorry, too.

I miss you terribly. I can't wait to come back home.

I miss you, too.

Look, I was thinking, when I get back, we can take a trip up the coast. Monterrey, Morro Bay…

That sounds nice, but I wish we could do it now. I wish we'd done it before.

Me, too.

God, I love you, baby.

I love you, too. I know you have to go. Goodb—

No, don't hang up yet. How are the kids?

Missing you. We all miss the daddy-man. But you have to go now. Because duty calls. And it always will. You have things to do. Important things.

No, wait! Sara! Wait!

I'll love you forever…

Sara!

He started awake, his hands still shaking. He'd been dreaming. Dreaming about Sara. Her touch, her beautiful eyes, even her slightly crooked smile. He'd screwed it up, and it was no one's fault but his. It had been time and past time to hang it up and fix things at home. The Teams could take care of themselves for a while. The pain in his throat interrupted his dream and, as he returned to full consciousness, a raging thirst asserted itself, driving all other concerns to the distant background.

His eyes felt like sandpaper. Harry blinked, trying to ease the discomfort. He turned his head, feeling a pillow crinkle under his neck, and the ambient light began to grow.

"Welcome back, Lieutenant," a warm tenor voice said.

It came from his right side, so he looked that way. First, he saw a small, opaque observation window. As his vision cleared, Harry noted the room included a few television-style monitors and the familiar shapes of medical equipment wrapped in curved beige plastic. He'd been in his share of hospital rooms, usually to check on a teammate who'd earned a bad luck medal. His eyes slowly tracked further, taking in a pair of flight-suited men standing at *his* bedside.

So, this time, he was the star of the show. Well, shit.

"Helicopter...shot...down?" he managed. "Hospital?"

"Yes," the taller of the two men replied, picking up a wired remote and pressing the button to slowly raise Harry's bed to a sitting position. As it smoothly whined upwards, the plain-faced attendant continued. "Your helo was shot down off Somalia. Nearly all of the crew and passengers were recovered. Can you hold this?"

He proffered a white plastic cup, and Harry leaned forward, carefully grasping it with both hands. He noticed in passing that rather than one of those embarrassing ass-less hospital smocks, he was fully dressed. In fact, his shirt sleeve was the same, familiar desert tricolor camo he'd worn in the Mog, right down to the modified pocket he'd asked Sara to sew onto the upper sleeve. After a long sip of cool water from the convenient straw, he leaned back and exhaled.

"Thanks, I really needed that," he croaked, looking at the speaker. The stranger looked vaguely familiar, though the bulky flight suit didn't match any American pattern he recognized. The gold oak leaves on the collar points were familiar, as was the Midwestern American accent. "Commander…"

"It's major, actually." The sandy haired man smiled. "Rodger Murphy. You and I were on the same Blackhawk. They woke me up a short while ago. We've got a bit of a system now, so if you let me give you some background, we can skip past the first ten or so questions. Okay?"

Harry looked at him suspiciously, then gave the room another once over. There were English labels here and there, but otherwise there was no information. No charts, no hospital PA system, not even a call button. Just a coat of gray paint, newly applied, by the smell.

"We?"

"Yes, we," Murphy replied with a smile and held up one hand. His shorter companion rolled his eyes and passed the major a small blue piece of paper. "I can tell from the squint in your eyes you're already figuring out this isn't a regular hospital room, and this isn't a normal recovery. I've been helping wake up paranoid, pissed off, and otherwise uncooperative military personnel for a week or so. Let me give you a basic data dump, then we can proceed to the more interesting questions. Ready?"

This definitely wasn't normal procedure for bringing someone out of deep sedation or a medically induced coma, Harry realized. This Major Murphy, or whatever his name really was, had it right. Harry surreptitiously flexed his arms and legs. No pain, no restraints.

Murphy's smile broadened and he held up his hand again. The second man placed another blue chit, grimacing.

"Of course, you could continue like this," Murphy said, as the second man scowled and folded his arms. "Captain Makarov has made a series of rather unwise wagers and you're making me plenty of drink chits, those being one of the few forms of currency we have at the moment. And to your unspoken questions: no, you're not restrained. Yes, you're medically recovered. Shall we proceed?"

Harry nodded warily, looking at both men. Drink chits? This was not your average reassuring medical speech. Were these guys the opposition? Could the Aideed militia even shop him out to...whoever these guys belonged too?

Harry took another pull on the straw to hide his confusion, but nodded assent. Murphy deferred to the shorter man with a "c'mon" gesture.

"Your *vertolet,* how you say, *'copter,* was shot down November 17, 1993," Makarov said with a heavy Slavic accent. Russian? It was a bit more slurred, sounding a bit like their guys who spent too long in the 'Stans. A Kazakh, maybe? And what the hell was he doing here?

Makarov made direct eye contact with Harry. "We still don't know who responsible, but the *'copter* carrying you and Major Murphy took two missiles. Crash was pretty spectacular. Killed copilot and crew chief. You were severely injured. You've received highly advanced medical treatment, but now only need the usual rest, healthy diet, and exercise. In fact, you're medically approved for duty. Clear so far?"

How long have I been here? Where's Sara?

"Have you informed my wife?" Harry asked, overcome with a sudden sense of urgency. Sara would be losing her mind. In fact, he was surprised she wasn't here right now, knowing how pushy she could be, especially where family was concerned. Singularly unimpressed with military protocol, she'd fight her way to his bedside if she had to. "How long have I been out? Where are we—Frankfurt? San Antonio?"

The expressions on both men changed to something a doctor might wear on the cusp of delivering a fatal prognosis.

Harry began to feel something akin to panic, though he steeled his emotions. What had happened to Sara? The creepy feeling he always got in combat was prickling up his spine.

"Who are you guys?" he demanded. "Who you with? Is this an Agency op? Why the hell am I in my field uniform in a hospital and who the fuck is the Russki?"

Murphy took over, with an apologetic glance at Makarov. "This is where it gets…weird, I'm afraid. Your recovery took a long time. A very long time. The U.S. didn't recover the survivors. The people who saved your life used an advanced cryogenic technique which preserved your uniform, your equipment, everything. There's no easy way to say this, so I'll just say it. The shoot down was a hundred and thirty-eight years ago. Today's date, Earth-style, is September 9, 2125."

Harry just stared at him. Then, involuntarily, started to laugh. It came out of nowhere, and he couldn't help it. This was the setup for every crappy sci-fi movie he'd ever heard of. He continued for a bit, looking at the men at his bedside. He expected them to get angry. Murphy just looked sad. Makarov managed a stolid indifference.

"What, no more betting?" Harry said sarcastically. "Come on, who do you work for? This is a set up. Time travel isn't real. Cryogenic tech isn't real. If you tried to pull a Disney on me, my brain would be torn apart by ice crystals, just like Walt's. Stop wasting my time and tell me what you want; otherwise, all you get is Tapper, Harold R., Lieutenant, U.S. Navy. 620-11-2129."

"Like Major said, we've been doing this for long time," Makarov answered, moving toward the window. "Is easier to show than tell." He touched a light switch on the window frame, and it blinked into transparency.

Stars were slowly drifting past. Stars against a deep, perfect black. There was a wall of gray and brown rock filling a third of the field of view. As he watched, it slowly moved, no, rotated. Craters and lines were visible. The moon? After a few more moments, he discerned he was looking at one end of a rocky cylinder, immense in size. A construct, reminiscent of NASA's old Spacelab, was slowly emerging from a shadowed opening at one end of the cylinder. Harry struggled to get a sense for scale. He recognized a human figure in a bulky looking, helmeted coverall, sitting astride a girder that made up part of the vehicle, if that's what it was. It was a spacesuited person, Harry belatedly realized. The entire scene snapped into focus. The rotating cylinder was more than a couple klicks long and half as thick.

The decidedly non-aerodynamic ship carefully emerging had an industrial look, covered in a mixture of silver and white panels, some pristine and some stained and scratched. Piping and cableways snaked through trestles.

A solar panel array, recognizable anywhere, slowly swept into view. It was tended by a tiny, delta winged craft, colored white and black. Though it was much further away, Harry realized this ship was the size of 747 wide-body jet. Harry watched them slowly swing past the window. Then the limb of a planet swam into view, by degrees. It was banded in swirling clouds like Jupiter, but it wasn't from the Solar System, unless Jupiter had changed colors to include purple and yellow.

He was *on* a space station.

No. Impossible. His head began to swim, and he shook it hard, before looking back toward the two men.

"This overview is what you SEALs like to call the mission summary—first, you're aboard a spaceship, the Dornaani cruiser *Olsloov*," Murphy said, carefully pronouncing the unfamiliar word. *Alls-sluv*. "The Dornaani are an allied, non-Terran species who are very advanced. We're docked next to a space habitat, that moon-looking thing you see out the window. It's run by another branch of humanity, refugees really. Also, there's an interstellar war on, and you were recovered from a stolen cache of cryogenically suspended humans, mostly men and mostly military, kidnapped out of conflict zones on Earth starting about two hundred years ago, ending in the early two thousands. The folks who did it are another alien species, the Ktor, and they were using us to do some dirty work they could blame on Earth. The only way we get to go home is to work together, kick Ktor ass, and win this war. The details will take days to absorb. What do you think so far?"

Harry returned to looking out the window. The solar array had rotated out of sight and the swirling surface of the gas giant now spanned the view.

"T-trick," Harry said, almost stuttering the word. "Some kind of trick. That's some kind of special effects. One of those new rear-projection big screen televisions. You're trying to fool me—"

"Well, we're taught American SEALs are stubborn, selected for it, in fact," Makarov said, shrugging. "So, reaction is no surprise. Next step we use for tough cases is suit them up for EVA. So far, weightlessness and new planet convince everyone. We need to do this, or can we save some time?"

Harry was staring at the sharply drawn shadow creeping up the curved sweep of the hull plating outside.

This can't be real.
This can't be real.
THIS ISN'T REAL.

His thinking brain was trying to pick out flaws in the computer-generated simulation. Meanwhile, his hindbrain was desperately trying to control his rising gorge.

His efforts at rationalization failed first by a narrow margin, and then he vomited over the side of his bed, splashing the shoes of both men.

"Ha!" Harry heard Makarov exclaim, just before Harry's gut convulsed a second time. "I predict correctly. Give last chit back, Major."

* * *

Harry had taken over a table in the corner of the refectory serving this quadrant of the habitat. The Lost Soldiers, as the Terrans called themselves, ate together. What their mostly human hosts who ran the station, the SpinDogs, thought about it was a mystery since the two groups didn't readily mix.

During the mandatory orientation and safety training arranged by the SpinDogs, Harry and a company's worth of the Lost Soldiers had trooped for hours through myriad passageways, engineering spaces, and general-use compartments and had still only visited a fraction of the station. The visit for his motley group had been comprehensive, equipping Harry with an appreciation for the engineering feat represented by the SpinDogs' cylindrical asteroid, which had been cored out and converted into a difficult-to-detect space habitat. Each end of the station housed heavy equipment, docking bays, and power generation, leaving the multi-decked center section to house living quarters, light industrial work, hydroponics, and the like. This was the beating heart of the habitat. Even one such deck was several times larger than the biggest aircraft carrier ever built by his country, and yet the degree to which the SpinDogs maximized the productivity of every available cubic meter pushed home the point that their growth had outstripped their capacity. The addition of less than a hundred Terrans to a population of almost one hundred thousand was still a strain, more so because of Major Murphy's insistence his team be housed together, isolated from the general population.

Of course, all of that followed a week of acclimatization to the new reality. The world Harry had known was beyond reach, and the new Earth was almost as unknowable. Current reports painted an Earth very different from the 1990s. Borders had been redrawn, and he barely recognized what passed for political parties. The newly woken soldiers were mostly American, but there were enough Aussies, Afghanis, Vietnamese, and Russians to give their group an international feel. Of course, that mattered hardly at all to other species, one of which Harry had already seen in person—the short, gray bipeds running the Dornaani cruiser. Harry had learned there were at least five intelligent species in contact with humanity. The combat videos of the alien invasion of Earth revealed giant roach-like insects and bipedal anteater-werewolf hybrids. Bizarrely, negotiations were now underway to convert both of those alien races into allies while Earth entered a fight against the mostly human group which had kidnapped the Lost Soldiers out of their own time.

And of course, the worst reality of all: Harry couldn't stop thinking about his irredeemable failure, the loss of his family. The number one thing he had finally sworn to do, to be present for Sara and the kids, was now forever beyond his reach.

The former SEAL heard the soft footsteps of a person approaching his makeshift workspace and a sudden, powerful wave of irritation surged, blanketing his self-pity. Every six hours, he had to pack his work into a plastic crate while the space was used for its original purpose. A glance at his venerable Casio G-Shock confirmed he should have plenty of time left. With an hour to go until the next meal, he expected to be left alone unless there was an emergency, and he hadn't heard any of the alarms they'd memorized as the result of frequent drills.

"Harry, do you have a moment?" asked a now-familiar voice.

A glance over his shoulder confirmed his new boss, if that's what he was, was approaching, an insulated stainless-steel mug in hand.

"No problem, sir," Harry replied, smiling as genuinely as he could. He felt the anger rekindling itself in the wake of his initial irritation, and shoved it back down, hard. The guy in charge was entitled to interrupt whenever he felt like it, especially since he wasn't here by choice, either. Harry twisted in his seat, lifting a stack of z-folded printouts, old-style notebooks, and a variety of maps from the bench across from him.

"I've told all of you to call me Rodger, or Roj, if you prefer," Murphy replied with a smile as he slid onto the bench. "While we're a military outfit, we're all professionals, and I'm not enough of a little tin god to insist on unctuous military protocol."

"Okay, Roj," Harry replied, wrinkling his brow unconsciously.

"How goes your mission prep?"

"Well…"

"Let me guess," Murphy replied, raising one hand. "You're underwhelmed with your choice of teammates. You're questioning the limitations on unit size. You keep asking yourself how this can possibly be the best option. Am I getting close?"

"Spot on," Harry said, schooling his face into neutrality. "Look, you're asking, right? This is actually a lot more complicated than the mission summary you gave me when I woke up. Let's pretend our people are successful getting over the loss of their families and everything they knew. I won't even mention the crap equipment we have to use. Let's assume I accept the restrictions the fu—our hosts are imposing on us. Bottom line, damn near everything depends on planetside locals we haven't yet met. And we'll be operating across some pretty crappy terrain, almost entirely on foot, for the first several phases."

Harry pushed aside more papers, this time on top of the table. He exposed a featureless, black-screened device he'd been given. He'd gotten over the vast differences from the IBM PC he'd last used in the 20th century and rapidly mastered the finger movements needed to control the legal document-sized, touch-operated screen.

"Here's what I mean."

A touch from a single thick finger illuminated the screen to reveal a grid of multicolored icons. He tapped a symbol shaped like a simplified, yet old-fashioned Mercator map projection. The planetary surface which blinked into existence showed the familiar swirl of clouds and blue ocean that might have been mistaken for Earth at a casual glance. However, there were only three main continents, two of which covered the poles. The equatorial region was mostly large islands, and those showed the light browns and sandy yellow colors of the deep desert. Harry used two fingers to orient the map on a point north of the equator, and then zoomed the view. He turned the datapad on its built-in stand so they both could see an area which included a mix of terrain ranging from grassy plains to rocky, channeled hills to outright desert.

"We insert via a high-risk orbital drop and land up to fifty klicks from the objective in order to avoid detection by the Kulsians, who have an established intelligence network, including aerial patrols." As Harry talked, he couldn't avoid thinking about how absurd the situation was, even as he pointed to each feature on the map. "After a long foot infil, I link up with tribes the SpinDogs *think* will be receptive to our plan. Once we've found the right bunch, I get to convince them, however I'm going to manage it, that they should work with us and allow me to train them. After which our merry band of hunter-gatherers plus yours truly perform local ops in order to gather more tribes to our forces. Then—and we still haven't reached the good part—our combined force preps for an assault landing with one—

that's *one*—shuttle to deliver the rest of the Lost Soldiers and we seize a modern mechanized column intact using nothing but infantry. If I'm anything but perfectly successful, I'm stuck on a planet where the opposition is entrenched and more than a bit pissed that unknown forces—which would be me—have killed dozens, maybe hundreds, of their people and sparked an insurgency. To top it off, the planet is turning into a goddamn oven in two years, inhabitable nowhere but at the poles—which are thousands of klicks from where I'm going to land. Forlorn hope—hell—it would be simpler and kinder to just eat a goddamned bullet!"

As he finished, Harry abruptly realized he'd almost yelled the last couple sentences. Raising his voice to a man, who, if he wasn't exactly his commanding officer, was certainly sufficiently in charge to have Harry tossed out an airlock.

"Got it out of your system?" Murphy asked, smiling thinly.

"I'm sorry, but—yeah. Sorry." Harry took a drink, ignoring the flat taste of water re-filtered countless times. It gave him something to do besides look at his boss.

"In case you haven't figured it out yet," Murphy said, his eyes cold, "this *is* a forlorn hope. I didn't ask for this. *None of us asked for this.* Yet here we are. The facts of the case are not in dispute and the hard truths I've previously explained to each member of this team still stand. The world we knew is literally history. The family you were lucky enough to have in 1993 is gone. Somewhere on Earth you may have adult great-grandchildren, but you're not a memory to them. Hell, you aren't even a book report for some great-great-grandkid's school assignment. The people, and hell, even the *culture*, we knew are as dead as they believed you to be after you were declared missing. We're all in the same boat, and time has fucking well moved on. Are you clear?"

"Yes, sir," Harry said miserably, rubbing his forehead hard enough to draw the skin white across his brow.

"Are you fucking clear?" Murphy asked again, almost hissing.

There was a long pause.

"Yeah. I'm clear," Harry replied again, this time looking the other man in the face.

"Then you will stop feeling sorry for yourself," Murphy replied more normally. He drummed his fingers on the tabletop for a few moments. "We've all lost everything. Maybe we can get back and maybe we can't. All that's left is hope and each other. Some of the Lost are so broken that they can't cope, not now and maybe never. When we picked who we were bringing out of cryo-suspension, I thought you could hack it. Was I wrong?"

"I can hack it," Harry said, instantly. Being able to endure anything was the closest thing to a SEAL religion there was. Or had been, anyway.

"So, we get to figure out how to do the impossible," Murphy said, warming to the topic. "The SpinDogs won't risk everything by landing in force. Their support for large-scale surface operations and directly confronting the Kulsians is contingent on a demonstration of our superior warfighting skills. A *successful* demonstration."

There was an uncomfortable silence. Harry felt guilty, not as much for losing his cool, even momentarily, but because he wasn't living up to his image of himself.

"You ever heard of Murphy's Law?" the major asked.

"Practically live by it, in the Teams," Harry answered automatically. Everyone who spent enough time in the military knew that whatever could go wrong, would go wrong. A deep understanding that the universe was waiting to trip you up had spawned several other sayings among those who took up the profession of arms.

"Two is one, one is none" and *"tracers work both ways"* as well as the ever popular *"fifteen minutes prior to fifteen minutes prior"* mantra intended to promote punctuality—and many others—were the half-humorous watchwords by which modern soldiers lived. All were intended to counter the reality of Murphy's Law.

Harry suddenly and belatedly made the connection to his new boss' surname.

"Glad to hear it," Murphy said decisively. "We're going to break that law. We're going to plan ahead for things to go wrong in order to make sure they end up right. That starts with you. You are going to come up with a plan making Murphy's Law a problem for the other guy. We're going to be a sharp, unexpected stick in the opposition's tender spots. Now, have you settled on who's going with you?"

"This is going to be a variation on an exchange training mission, so whoever goes with me should have worked with indigs before," Harry answered, using the abbreviated form of "indigenous" to refer to the local population. "This isn't a job for junior cadre. Rodriguez is the best candidate. He also has the best Ktor language rating of the available senior enlisted."

Most of the Lost Soldiers had spent days in the Dornaani cruiser's virtual reality bay, receiving accelerated Ktor language training at ten-to-one time compression. The unpleasant experience had left them with persistent migraines for a few days. However, they were all now conversant, though not perfectly fluent, with the dominant language of the system.

In addition to his language score, Rodriguez's folio called out several missions in the sixties with the Cambodians, the South Vietnamese, and the Hmong. On the personal side, it highlighted his readiness to rebel against authority figures, his womanizing, and the resulting children in Saigon, Manila, and elsewhere, which struck him as a bit odd, until Murphy explained something of the Ktoran preoccupation with genetics. He was also suspected of having fragged a newly promoted Army officer after that man's decisions had led to the death of Rodriguez's best friend in-country.

Speaking of which, Harry had initially been shocked at the detail in the personnel folders of the men from which he could choose. There was a lot more there than the basics of a military service record. It was a cross section of their life, including family details, bank statements, and school transcripts. It was probably more information than the subjects had even assembled for themselves. Which meant...

Might as well get it all out on the table.

Harry tapped the personnel folders he'd reviewed for this operation. "Roj, I'm betting the British spook—the one you introduced to all of us before he beat feet on that fancy alien ship—he's your source of information on everyone, including me."

"No bet."

"Then you know why I was on the helicopter." Harry made it a statement, not a question.

"I know, Harry," Murphy answered, nodding. "And, frankly, I can't see the conditions we're under are going to help. If you haven't figured it out, the group *Olsloov* left behind were the last to be roused from cold sleep for one reason or another. We weren't woken by the Ktor, and we weren't initially revived by our own allies. The files the Dornaani recovered were remarkably complete. Your decorations, correspondence, counseling records, everything. Bottom line: your last CO could afford to send you back stateside because he had options. I don't. What's more, you and I are from very nearly the last batch of Terrans the Ktor kidnapped. We share the same military and cultural context, which means a lot. And, like you said, if you screw this up, you're gonna be stuck down there. Seems like pretty good motivation, if you ask me."

Harry watched as the senior man took another pull from his mug. It trembled very slightly as he sat it down, and Murphy grimaced.

"As long as you're down there, check to see if they have anything better than this dishwater tea."

"I'm hoping for some coffee, Roj," Harry said, extending an olive branch.

"Hell, if they have real coffee, I'll come retrieve you myself."

* * * * *

Chapter Three

Volo squinted at the horizon, trying to match the outline of the rolling hills with the terrain relief on the expedition map. Ignoring the pack straps cutting into his shoulders, he glanced down at the plastic-coated map to confirm the bearing of the three peaks dominating the view to the east during their march. Although he'd begun the second morning of their hike with a precise location fix, courtesy of the just-emplaced Dornaani stealth-sats, he needed two, or preferably three, of the very small satellites to be in line-of-sight at the same time. Another such intermittent conjunction would occur this night, so navigation wasn't the top issue. His little group's location was the current problem.

The automated evasion by their drop capsules had placed them far away from the usual range of their trading partners on the surface. This meant much more travel on foot and an associated delay. It also meant considerably more discomfort.

Before turning to face his companions, he carefully groomed his expression into neutrality, erasing any sign of the discomfort his tailored boots or borrowed Terran backpack were inflicting. His brother Stabilo, the most recent Zobulakos to have landed on R'Bak, had cautioned Volo to rigorously condition himself in the high-gee pod of the *Second Spin*. At the time, Volo believed his brother's outlandish claims about conditions on the surface were exaggerations designed to deter the youngest of their family, or even plant the seed of failure in Volo's mind, leaving the way open for Stabilo to remain the favored son. The unexpected arrival of the Dornaani cruiser and its cargo of rootstock humans had radically accelerated the schedule for Volo's first visit to the surface, and, while his wind was good, the soreness of his feet and joints was distracting at best, and potentially a dangerous weakness at worst. Such was not the way of their family, where personal strength vied with utility and efficiency as the most prized qualities.

"We're proceeding as planned," Volo said, looking over his shoulder to the next man. The over-muscled Terran officer had paused several steps behind him, endlessly looking to both sides. "I updated the satlink with your situation report. We should get a reply tonight."

"Sounds good," Tapper replied, nodding but otherwise showing no expression. Establishing some rapport with the archaic humans was important to Volo's mission, but the larger man, the officer, had been difficult to approach. Volo watched him scratch his neck, and, unbidden, his own dirty collar began to itch almost unbearably. Instead of giving in to the weakness, he turned to continue the march, suppressing the desire to scratch. Volo despised Tapper's casual acceptance of the sweat and dirt coating them both. It was a reflection of the Terran's barbarous people, who, by their own admission, mostly still scrabbled on the surface of their homeworld.

Volo's father, the Arko Primus of the entire habitat, regarded these humans as a potential resource even more valuable than the centuries-old space wreckage the SpinDogs used as their principle source of refined alloys. Finding a rich hulk was the sort of event that could guarantee the succession of a favored heir. These Terrans, and their patrons, the Dornaani, might change everything, and the success of this mission would leapfrog Volo ahead of all his siblings.

Better, the Terrans were terribly naive and had accepted everything the Primus had told them. Of course, most of the facts about the millennium-old conflict between Kulsis and R'Bak were not in dispute. The two halves of the binary star system had been sought out by three separate waves of Ktoran outcasts. Volo's people, the SpinDogs, had been part of the second wave, and were surprised to find both systems already inhabited. The greatest power was on Kulsis, the habitable planet of the main system. Fortunately, there was no sign that the modest Kulsian presence in space was poised for journeys to the companion system, so the second wave settled on R'Bak. Although the details were sketchy, the later generations of those settlers were split by disputes, one of which led to a sizeable group being sent off-planet: the ancestors of the SpinDogs. Given the unpleasant relations with their dirtside cousins, Volo's forebears elected to build their communities in secret locations. This protection against local aggression was ultimately what spared them from the out-system depredations that began about a century later. And so, the small SpinDog civilization remained hidden, sheltering on asteroids scattered among the uninhabitable planets of the ecliptic, biding its time.

Volo suppressed a smile. What the Terrans didn't know was that the death of the Matriarch at the hands of the Kulsians was an opportunity for his family, and for Volo personally. That these Terran visitors felt partially responsible was a useful lever he would use to steer their behavior. Once he linked up with the tribe which had previously traded with the SpinDogs, he could exploit the good relationship built by his father and siblings on previous excursions to the surface to sway the Sarmatchani toward the Terran's plan. The natural suspicion the tribesmen had for his people was nothing compared to their visceral hate for the Kulsians and their satraps. Their instinctive distrust of the Terrans would help Volo establish and maintain control.

Volo paused again at the top of yet another hill and wiped his sweaty face. He looked around skeptically, but the terrain they'd been traversing offered little of interest. He glanced over his shoulder again. Both Terrans were ascending stolidly, apparently unaffected by the absurdly high gravity and the increasing heat.

Whether these visitors could actually defeat the Kulsians or not remained to be seen. A win would interrupt the cycle of destruction wrought by the Kulsians' "harvest" and the surface turmoil caused by the weather effects of the two stars at periastron. A loss could still mean a chance to directly ally with the Dornaani, once all the Terrans had conveniently died, of course. Either way, Volo would squeeze every opportunity from his temporary position of advantage and become the one to succeed his father.

* * *

The sand shifted under Harry's boots, making each stride that much more difficult as he followed several meters behind Volo. Despite his muscular frame and what he'd been promised was a gravity slightly lower than Earth's, the weight of the pack was an uncomfortable irritant and his back was really starting to ache. The well-worn Vietnam-era ALICE ruck was not the most ergonomic bit of kit Harry had used, carrying most of the weight too low on his spine, but more American equipment from that era was available than any other. Rodriguez had accepted his gear without comment, but the last time Harry had seen some of this stuff, it had been gathering dust on the shelves of an Army surplus store. Out of long habit, he'd slung his equally dated M-14 rifle so he could keep one hand on the grip, patrol fashion. Harry watched ahead as the SpinDog followed the narrow game trail winding through the swaying, hip- to shoulder-high yellow saw grass. Over the course of the day, the earlier sparse forest had largely thinned as the little party hiked further west. Occasional bare trunks of dead trees poked up here and there from the tall, dry grass. Some past violent weather event had shaped the sand into a series of rolling hills, each rising as much as fifty meters high, and, while the trail they followed mostly wound between successive ridges, they inevitably spent a lot of time going up and down.

Apart from looking straight ahead or down toward his boots, Volo seemed unconcerned with their surroundings.

Harry paused for a moment to look over his shoulder. An equal distance behind, Rodriguez had also stopped, scanning their back trail, which reassured Harry nearly as much as Volo's casual manner irritated him. After a short interval, Rodriguez turned and continued, and Harry caught his eye while making the hand signal for a rally point. After receiving a nod in return, Harry lengthened his stride to close the gap to the lead member of their little group.

"Volo, we'll take a water break," Harry told their guide, who was stopped, consulting a partially folded plastic map. If Volo was unhappy to be using the same weapon that Harry carried, instead of the sleek carbines Harry had seen on *Second Spin*, he wasn't showing it. The nonchalant way Volo had slung his M-14 backwards, muzzle-down from one shoulder, allowed the SpinDog to use both hands. It also increased the time needed to deploy the weapon.

Harry bit back a caustic remark and watched Volo as he looked up the ascending slope of the track, then to the horizon ahead, and back to the map, consulting some spidery hand-written notes on the margin, as he'd periodically done throughout their march. He certainly wasn't in any hurry.

"How much further to the rendezvous coordinates?" Harry prompted. "I'd like to stop while there's enough light to make camp."

"It's dusk already," the slightly built young man replied, looking at his wristcom to double-check some reading. He didn't like what he saw and shook his head. "Midday tomorrow, perhaps the following day. The automated evasion response during our drop pushed our landing further north and east than we'd hoped. This morning, I had a solid microsat position, but now I must estimate. We're in the harvest fief claimed by the J'Stull, satraps to Kulsis, but they rarely venture this far from their cities. We seek a branch of the Sarmatchani who are kin to the group we trade with at the poles. They'll be found in this direction."

"So as long as it's still these Sarmatchani we link up with, it's all good then," Rodriguez said as he strode up, making the statement a question.

Harry looked at the NCO, wondering how the man was dealing with the impossibility of this situation. Rodriguez absentmindedly worked a bright orange plastic toothpick in his jaws as his eyes continued to look restlessly opposite the direction Harry was facing. His rifle moved to match his eyes, dipping now and again as the experienced sergeant kept the muzzle from flagging his teammates. "If they're expecting company, I mean?"

"The Sarmatchani are tribal and don't recognize a formal central authority," Volo replied. "They agree on little but their enmity for the satraps of Kulsis. They are good fighters, and the local Sarmatchani know every track around every hill in their territory. They may be watching already."

"If they see us, why don't they come meet us?" Harry asked, tilting his canteen up and swigging some warm water.

"It's their way," Volo answered calmly, folding the map closed. "We can't precisely schedule our visits, but we do land at regular intervals, when it's safe to trade. They watch for the J'Stull and guard their territory fiercely against competing clans. They will see us."

The SpinDogs land at regular intervals?

"Wait a minute," Harry said, fighting the instant and familiar surge of anger. "Your people routinely land on the surface? Why the hell did we do that crazy insertion then?"

With every word, Harry felt the heat of his rage begin to fill the channels and runnels lying under his otherwise calm exterior. Like a pusher who recognized every weakness in the addict, the rage soothed Harry's fear of the consequences if he gave in. It reminded him of every time he'd been let down or betrayed, cut, or stung. And here was another indig, withholding information while demanding everything. Harry struggled to keep his tone even because he wouldn't yield to the temptation. He couldn't. Control was his friend; rage his enemy.

"You've been instructed," Volo answered, pale eyes narrowing as he omitted the obvious qualifier *"you ignorant savage,"* "The Second Exodate, *my people*, must conceal our very existence, lest we share the fate of all on R'Bak. The raiders from Kulsis have sent their advance parties, as they have done each time our stars draw close to one another, making travel possible. So extra caution would have been required, regardless. And then, uninvited, your people intervened in the matter of the Matriarch, drawing unwanted attention just at the time when discretion was most important."

Harry's rage didn't like the youngster's tone. The SpinDogs had briefed their network on-planet, and Harry knew they'd landed before. But routine landings had never been mentioned. What else had his so-called allies left out? He tried to think of the most constructive reply while suppressing the adrenaline which always accompanied his familiar, unbidden fury. He squeezed the wooden pistol grip of his rifle to hide his anger and stared at Volo, who insolently returned his glare. Harry noted Rodriguez's concerned glance and flicked his offhand that way.

Deal with this.

"Look, Volo, we're sorry about this whole mess, but we didn't know you SpinDogs were in the system," Rodriguez said placatingly. "And once we figured it out, we tried to help out, save your queen—"

"She was no queen. *She was the Matriarch.* And she perished!"

"—and besides, the boss and I were still asleep when it happened," the sergeant finished his attempt at smoothing things over. "You didn't ask for this, and we didn't ask for this. But it is what it is."

"Yes, I know about you Sleepers," Volo replied, firmly jamming the map into a thigh pouch. Harry could tell he was only partially mollified. "We used a similar suspension technique to bridge the distance from our parent system. Though much of our history is lost, we SpinDogs remember how the other Ktor cast us out hundreds of years ago. Ktor technology is now far ahead of our own, and the

Kulsians have a fleet whose size is possible because of their planetary control—which is the reason we must remain unseen. With your ship gone, we cannot directly challenge them in space."

Harry took a deep breath. He dismissed his anger by careful stages, which finally and sullenly retreated beyond immediate thought. He flexed one hand and nodded thanks to Rodriguez, who returned it before turning around and resuming his scan.

"Your people and mine have agreed to work together," Harry said, fully back in control.

Harry had worked with indigenous personnel several times during the course of many deployments. Panama, Kuwait, Somalia; it was always the same. Each one was so sure they had all the answers. They just wanted the Americans to fix their problems, give them funding and tech, and of course do it all for free, and then go away. But he had to work with these people, so he'd swallow his anger. Like he always did.

Almost always.

"Out of respect for your situation, we've agreed to proceed carefully and prove we can accomplish what we claim," he finished.

"Uh, sir?" Rodriguez called from behind them.

"Before conveniently departing, *your* ship destroyed the raiders' craft, their satellites, and their orbital habitat," Volo said angrily, putting both hands on his hips. "Those who escaped your attack know something is badly wrong. They have undoubtedly already changed their operational pattern while they await more of their comrades, who may arrive at any time. Even now, they warn their loyal satraps, seeking to turn every hand against those who have struck this blow. Against this change we must still protect the secret of our race. Thus, the space drop and this, admittedly, slow route to our rendezvous."

He gestured ahead.

"That is why we took the time to cover the descent pods with parachutes," he added tartly. "That is why the LZ was so distant from our previous landing points, just in case we'd been detected before. Now, if you are sufficiently reassured, Lieutenant," he said, turning to continue the march, "we should press on."

"Hey!" Rodriguez said a little more loudly. "You officers want to take a look at this and maybe argue later?"

Harry glanced up immediately. One of the dead trees scattered about stood close to the track, extending a few meters above the waving grass. As he watched, a pair of dark eyes blinked, and the motion served to reveal a small gray form, the outline of which blended into the bark. The middle of the creature seemed to pulse, and a soft hooting sound carried around the immediate area. Small teeth projected from the seam of its jaw, no bigger than the last joint of Harry's little finger.

"Well, that's hardly an emergency," Harry said, eyeing the meter-sized creature. "We'll just skirt around to one side."

But then he noticed Volo's reaction, and stopped. A moment earlier he'd been angry and determined, but now the SpinDog had frozen.

"Quiet!" Volo whispered. He began to slowly reach for the slung weapon with one trembling hand, before he stopped and let his arm gradually descend to his side. "It's not alone."

Harry scanned both sides of the track, but the grass concealed possible dangers.

"It's not very large," he said softly. "Is it venomous?"

"No," Volo answered. "That's a juvenile, forced into sentry duty by the adults. They get much bi—"

The creature hooted again, and this time, deeper calls sounded all around the three humans. Perhaps ten meters away, a much larger version of the sentry's head, reminiscent of a Terran bat, slowly rose from the grass until it was nearly at shoulder level with Harry. Two dark eyes sparkled with intelligence above membranous slits which pulsed slowly. Furred ears projected from each side of the head, swiveling in concert to orient on the humans. Four paired tusks nearly as long as Harry's forearm hung from the bottom of the skull. Stained the same color as the grass, the tusks moved rhythmically as the creature chewed a mouthful of foliage. The hooting calls were repeated, more strident this time, and Harry was able to see they were emitted from the nasal slits, while the jaws ceaselessly ground together.

Harry instantly raised his rifle, flicking the safety off. His peripheral vision showed movement all around, and Harry could feel his sergeant switching his aim between targets as more of the creatures loomed into view on both sides.

"Aw, crap," Rodriguez said in a strained voice. "You seeing this?"

"Don't shoot!" Volo said, keeping his voice low and slowly stepping closer to Harry and laying a hand on top of his rifle. "They have no fear of men. There are dozens we can't see, and they are dangerous when roused; even larger predators leave these alone. Don't look in their eyes, it's a challenge. Don't make sudden movements. No loud noises—they will attack whoever makes the loudest sound. We don't want to provoke them."

"Boss?" Rodriguez said in a strained voice. "Make the call, Harry."

The nearest animal shuffled onto the track. It was massively built, and the nightmare head was perched above the hunched shoulders of a hyena. The gray fur was shaggy, dappled with darker spots down the flanks. The forelimbs had digits tipped with a shiny, keratinlike substance. Since Harry was looking downwards, he had a good view as the creature's knuckles took the weight of the muscular forequarters, splaying a little and sinking into the sandy track.

Heavy. Third of a ton, maybe more.

The troop leader used one paw to pound the ground, accompanied by a particularly loud hoot. Harry was confident he could shoot it several times before it closed the distance, but he had no idea what passed for a nervous system on this planet, nor did he know how large the troop was. Worse, the antique he was carrying held only twenty rounds of standard ball ammo, and if there was something less attractive than trying for a magazine change while wrestling with a tusked gorilla, it wasn't obvious at the moment. For a second, Harry thought wistfully of the CAR727 and the hundred round magazine he had carried in Somalia. It was probably somewhere on the now-departed *Olsloov*. The mysterious Mr. Nuncle, Murphy's boss, had been insistent about ammunition commonality and using the largest caliber rifle they had in numbers, which was the M-14. At least he'd been able to snag two of the squad support variants—the M14E3—for himself and Rodriguez.

On the other hand, Volo might know what he was talking about. Harry struggled for a moment and then decided. At some point, he had to trust him. Exhaling, he kept his eyes down, but maintained his weapon at the low ready.

"Okay, now what?" he asked Volo, murmuring softly.

"They're migrating, with young," Volo replied, still keeping his voice low. "It makes them aggressive. We very slowly back away from the pack leader. Stay together, move quietly, and don't make any quick or threatening motions."

"What the hell is a threatening motion to an alien baboon-bat?" Harry heard Rodriguez mutter. However, the noncom also looked down and slowly backed away as all three retraced their steps.

One animal, larger than the sentry but still much smaller than the troop master, shuffled forward, hooting and raising its upper body off the ground before slapping the turf with loud thuds. The display was probably calculated only to intimidate. However, the newcomer was stirring the passions of the increasingly loud troop and more animals knuckle-walked into direct line-of-sight, slapping the ground and hooting. The sentry began shaking the tree, and the dry limbs clattered together.

Harry resigned himself to opening fire. He'd try for head and neck shots and hope for the best. But, before he could do so, the troop master moved forward with unexpected agility. Two quick steps brought him to his target and a blow from one massive forearm drove the smaller, louder animal into the ground. The tusks of the larger beast clacked together as it bellowed a crashing challenge or command. The rest of the pack was suddenly quiescent, scuttling back into the grass and out of view. Just as suddenly as it had attacked the upstart, the lead animal appeared to calm. The giant remained watchfully poised on one forelimb, which rested on the back of the downed smaller animal, but it used the other to rip a clump of vegetation from the ground. It stuffed the morsel into its neck-mouth and resumed the important business of eating, all the while observing the humans.

Maintaining control, check. *I hear you, big guy.*

Harry continued to step slowly away, while the pack leader remained in the center of the track, quietly watching the humans disappear back up the darkening track.

* * *

"Sitting around a campfire on an alien planet might be the weirdest thing I've ever done on an op, *sir,*" Rodriguez said, in English. "But it ain't the alien planet that bugs the shit out of me, it's the damn fire. Breaks every rule I've ever heard of, *sir.*"

Harry raised his eyebrows. *When your experienced NCO starts "sirring" you in the field, he isn't being polite, he's communicating something. Pointedly.*

The two men had gone for a short walk around their perimeter, getting oriented and accustomed to the differences in the appearance of nearby terrain as darkness enveloped their site. Both were professionals and knew without the need for discussion that getting a feel for their immediate surroundings at night would prevent false alarms and provide a corresponding advantage in a true crisis. The blackness wasn't absolute. R'Bak's tiny moons and the brilliant night constellations were still shining through the light cloud cover. Harry looked up and considered the empty sky with a pang of homesickness.

Helluva lot darker than the high desert in California, or Saudi for that matter.

He shrugged it off.

Mission first. Whine later.

Both men were trying to preserve their night vision by keeping their backs oriented towards the fire which Volo was occasionally poking with a handy stick. Rodriguez's unspoken question deserved an answer.

"Always show your enemies what they expect to see," Harry explained. "Out here, anyone skipping a fire is trying to hide. Someone who's trying to hide is someone who might be dangerous. Anyone who sees this fire will figure we're just another party of hide-hunters and not particularly interesting."

Rodriguez answered with a noncommittal grunt, navigating around a cluster of thick-stemmed, thorny plants which they had learned to avoid.

"Last night, we were still close to the drop capsules," Harry said, patiently, ignoring the sudden flare of aggravation at the NCO's non-answer. "Volo says we're firmly in tribal territory now, and a fire makes us easier for the Sarmatchani to find, which is the entire point of the exercise.

"You say so."

"Hold up, Marco," Harry ordered, trying to draw the sergeant out. "If you've got a feeling, tell me. I read about your ops. Your old team was more than half South Vietnamese. You've worked with more indigs than I have, and more closely. Do you think we can trust these people?"

"Yeah, I ran a bunch of ops into Indian Country in sixty-six, sixty-seven and again last year..." Rodriguez stopped suddenly, no doubt realizing that he was referring to a time more than a century past. Then he picked up the thread again. "Anyhow, they all went pretty well and SOG always composed the team with more ARVNs than Americans," he continued, pronouncing the abbreviation for the soldiers from the Army of Republic of Vietnam as a single word: *Ar-vin*.

Harry knew about the ARVNs and he knew about SOG. The work of the early special operators from the Military Assistance Command-Vietnam, Studies and Observation Group or MACV-SOG was—had been—legend inside SOCOM.

"The brass wanted to use the lowest number of Americans they could get away with. So last op, we get inserted by an ARVN Huey, not one from AirCav. And that's the op where ST UTAH never came back."

"And?" Harry prompted after a long pause. "What happened, exactly?"

"This time, the whole Viet Cong army was waiting," Rodriguez said, looking straight ahead. "We got rolled up even before the sound of the helo faded. We tried to di-di out of there, fought like hell, but half of us were blown away in the first two minutes. We got trapped in this little draw in the stinking jungle, not even a hundred yards from the insert LZ. Leaves, twigs, and shit raining down over our heads from all the fire going through the trees, covering the dead and wounded, sticking to the blood and the open holes showing through their gear."

Rodriguez paused again. Without looking directly at his teammate, Harry could sense that NCO was reliving the scene again, as fresh as the moment that it happened. He let the sergeant resume when he was ready.

"Bao, the last ARVN, was on the radio, trying to yell for a dust-off over the noise. Behind me, Steve was screaming, trying to stuff his guts back in, knowing he was gonna die lying in the dirt of the A-Shau valley. Then the shooting stops, all at once. You could hear the damn birds chirping. Some freaky dude in shades and a suit just appears, standing right there in the mud with us, offers us a way out but we had to decide right then. Next thing I know, I wake up on a goddamned spaceship, and two weeks later I'm looking at a strange sky that don't have no real moon in it, and all my men are gone. The files I got from the English spook say the two other guys extracted from UTAH got wasted fighting for the Ktor on the planet before this one. Same logs say the intel weenies back at the puzzle palace in Da Nang figured one of the ARVN air crew shopped our team to the VC a couple days before the op. 'Course, no way to know for sure. I'm here, now."

No way to know for sure: isn't that *the truth.*

Harry was looking up at the night sky. At some point during Rodriguez's story, Harry slipped back onto the Blackhawk for the ride out of Mog. The breeze of the slipstream, still hot despite the altitude and the speed of the helo. Electronic alarms suddenly blaring, the sound of the straining engine and the shaking, bucking airframe. The white face of the crew chief. An instant to think of Sara. The kids. An explosion. Then a kaleidoscope of sea-sky-sea—blackness.

Rodriguez turned to face Harry. The red light of the campfire several meters away danced across his face.

"Thing is, these teams of locals, soldiers, and spooks and shit only work good so long as everyone on the op has as much on the table as everybody else," he said before hawking and spitting downwind. "That alien dude over there, he looks like us, talks kinda like us, and maybe we can trust him. Maybe not. His ass seems to be on the line, same as ours. You and I want to go home. No way to know what he wants."

"I see it the same, Marco," Harry replied, holding out his hand for the sergeant, who took it firmly. "The way I figure it, it's you and me. The op is to get back to Earth."

"Roger that, El-Tee," Rodriguez said. "Back to Earth. So, yeah, I can put up with a campfire during an op. Or anything else. But who you gonna trust?"

* * *

"We can take turns keeping watch," Harry said to Volo, who was still sitting next to the small fire. "In case something happens."

"There's no need, Lieutenant," the SpinDog replied, preoccupied. He gently poked a dried branch into the flames and withdrew it before it caught. He repeated the motion. "Most animals on this planet won't willingly approach a fire. It's an ingrained behavior due to the Searing. As for the Sarmatchani, they will contact us or not."

"There are only three of us, and we will take turns staying awake," Harry said more firmly. "This isn't a negotiation. I'll go first and wake you up in two hours. When your two hours are up, you wake up Rodriguez. We repeat till morning and pick up the rotation tomorrow night. Got it?"

"As you wish." Volo never looked up from the fire.

Harry frowned, although he was glad to skip the expected argument. He watched the younger man stare into the flames.

"It's just a fire," Harry said, wondering about Volo's apparent fascination.

"I've never seen deliberately set fire before," he answered absently, holding his hands out, palms towards the dancing flames. "In person, that is. It's beautiful. And warm."

"How have you never seen a fire?" Harry asked, so startled his irritation was totally forgotten. He looked at Rodriguez, who had crossed his arms and turned to face outwards. "It's pretty basic. Everyone's seen a fire."

"*Intelligent* people don't allow fires in space habitats," Volo answered with a contemptuous look. "We conduct safety drills, but actual fire would be deadly in our habitats. Then there's the matter of fuel. Even if I could gather enough material from the farm compartment, it would be too wet to set alight easily, assuming I survived the wrath of the Chief of Hydroponics."

Harry had been genuinely curious, with no intention of setting Volo off, but now he had again aggravated his only connection to the locals, critical to the success of his mission. Before he could articulate a neutral response, Rodriguez spoke up.

"Makes sense," the sergeant said over his shoulder. Harry looked up and caught the NCO making little "take it easy" hand motions. "Didn't your brothers tell you what to expect?"

"The last person my father sent was my brother, Stabilo," Volo said, shrugging. "He told me about the gravity, of course. He talked about the richness of the land, where water and food were unrationed. He briefed me on the tribes we seek. We trade some simple tech and orbital survey information in exchange for samples of useful botanicals, other biological samples and information about the R'Baku satraps who've pledged fealty to Kulsis."

"Why haven't you allied with them outright?" Harry asked. "Couldn't you wipe the satraps off the planet and be ready for Kulsis yourself?"

"We are too few to control a planet while building the industrial base needed for orbital shipyards and munitions factories, all in the time available in a single cycle of the Searing," Volo replied, briefly looking up. "The raiders from Kulsis still have space superiority.

They could strike the planet and find our hidden stations in the asteroid clusters, and that would be the end. If your friends can help us seize the weapons and vehicle caches the Kulsians have seeded on the surface, we can interrupt the pattern that's kept us in hiding since our arrival. If we stop the cycle for even a single Searing, we would have a chance. We could finally control our own planet."

"You mean control along with the Sarmatchani, of course," Harry said wryly. "We need the tribesmen, and we need their willing help, Volo."

"Indeed," Volo said moodily, stirring the coals. He seemed to have completely missed Harry's semi-sarcastic remark. "Stabilo informed me he left on excellent terms with the local tribes and said they'd welcome our return."

"Is that so, Sky Man?" a new voice boomed from just beyond the firelight, opposite the side where both Harry and Rodriguez sat. Harry elected to slowly rise to his feet. After a beat, Volo began to stand, but a lance, its metal head gleaming orange and silver in the firelight, was abruptly laid across the SpinDog's shoulder. Footsteps crunched and a party of tall, hooded persons came into view. Volo sank back down, turning carefully to avoid the edge of lance head and still see behind him.

"You claim blood-ties with Stabilo the Liar?" the lance owner asked, stepping even closer. With an impatient shake, the tall man discarded the hooded robe which had obscured his face. Harry first noticed a magnificent graying mane and beard, only partially controlled with what appeared to be braids and fabric bands dyed some dark color. The man's face was lean and weathered, like shiny, tough leather. The protuberant nose and sharp cheekbones gave him the cast of a wolf. Bright, dark eyes peered out from under his beetled brow, meeting Harry's own, and they shone with intelligence and intent.

Harry held the newcomer's eyes and nodded toward Volo before he continued giving the man the once over, noting the fine white scars that crisscrossed the calloused hand holding the lance. With an effortless twitch, the shaft of the lance snapped vertical, coming to rest on a dark metal ferule. Several other robed figures stepped closer, all armed. Most carried lances and wore long knives, almost the length of short swords. Two cradled wooden-stocked firearms whose bores appeared wider than the width of Harry's thumb. None of them appeared particularly pleased to see the visitors.

"My name is Volo of the House Zobulakos," the SpinDog announced haughtily. Harry watched as his slender ally found his feet and made a show of brushing imaginary dust from his shoulder where the lance had rested.

Volo was defiant even in the face of drawn weapons; Harry had to give him points for style.

"I am here representing the esteemed friend to all Sarmatchani, my father, Arko Primus Heraklis Zobulakos. This is a mission of great importance. What honorless prole names my brother a liar and interferes with the will of the Primus? Tell me, that I might inform your chief of this insolence."

Harry tensed as two of the newcomers surged forward in angry reaction to the word "honorless," but the tall man interposed his lance, barring their way.

"Father!" the shorter one objected, throwing back her hood, revealing a sharp featured young woman. She'd drawn her blade and balefully eyed the SpinDog. "Let me teach this arrogant weakling about honor!"

"Nay, Stella," the broad-shouldered man said grimly. "Even my daughter must cleave to the law. This is a clan matter. And as to the stripling's question...

"I, hight Yannis al-Caoimhip ex-huscarlo, Patrisero of the Herdbane, First among the Sarmatchani," he went on, fixing his eyes first on Volo and then each of the Terrans. "I name Stabilo of the Sky People a liar, a cheat, and a coward. I call his people to account. Blood or treasure. At dawn tomorrow either will suffice."

Harry didn't say a word but heard a deep sigh from Rodriguez. These were the allies he'd been sent to find, all right. Just like every other joint operation with indigs, it was SNAFU.

Murphy's Law was in still in effect.

* * * * *

Chapter Four

I'm not too sure about this.
"Are you sure about this?" Rodriguez asked in English, standing a pace behind Harry. "I'm not particularly bad with a knife, but that boy looks like he's been to school."

Opposite them, waiting patiently in the wan pre-dawn light, was a broad-chested young man, perhaps twenty years old or so, if Harry was any judge. He'd been the male half of the two young people flanking the clan chief the night before, and his resemblance to the man in charge was unmistakable. An inch or two taller than Harry's own six feet, the younger man stood confidently, having shed his rifle and pack. Unlike Harry's camos, he wore simple trousers and a long-sleeved shirt, both of a grayish leather. The material was gathered below the knees and elbows with broad leather wraps, and his dark brown, shoulder-length hair was likewise bound. Behind him stood his sister, the one who'd indicated a desire to show Volo his own guts the previous night. As Harry watched, she passed a long, gleaming knife to her brother. The wooden handled weapon was shaped like a patcha skinning knife, and the drop point looked unsharpened above the tip, suggesting it was a slashing weapon.

The four of them were surrounded by the rest of the tribe, which stood inside a circle bounded by four large, wooden carts. The length of a prairie schooner, they were built with surprising skill, using a variety of metals for reinforcement and decoration. More than eighty meters away, a few of the younger members watched the clan's massive beasts of burden crop the short grass and roots in the ground. The animals were a peculiar cross between reptile and mammal. They resembled Earth's Komodo dragons, had those extinct beasts been covered in a scaled hide colored with alternating bands of tan and olive or stood shoulder high to a man, massing a couple of tons each. The creatures sported neck fringes they erected and shook when upset or aggressive, which seemed to be most of the time. They frequently whistled and bugled at their handlers, usually when the packs were loaded or when animals spotted a bit of choice forage. According to the chief, the whinnies, as they were called, would also eat anything and were sensitive to the smell of blood. Despite their objections, the youngsters along on the expedition didn't get to watch the impending duel, but had to tend the beasts instead.

"We need these folks, or the mission is already over," Harry said, looking away from the whinnies and back to his teammate. "Our kid, as touchy an asshole as he is, isn't used to the gravity yet and doesn't have much in the way of fighting skills, so if he dies on the little giant's knife, we risk the SpinDog' support. If we shoot our way clear, we're done. This duel is the only way I can see to get the mission done. And I'm not going to order you to do something I'm not particularly glad to do myself. So yeah, I'm sure."

Heh, listen to your pulse pounding already.

Okay. Mostly sure.

"If you waste Sonny, Daddy probably won't be inclined to go with our plan."

"Yeah, I'll try to remember."

"Well, then, remember the first rule of a knife fight," Rodriguez cautioned him before handing over the Gerber BMF Harry had carried in Somalia and now on R'Bak.

"What's that, Marco?"

"Losers die. Winners di-di to the field hospital. Only we ain't got a hospital."

The tribal shaman, or medicine woman, or whatever she was, stepped between the two, cutting off the smart-assed retort Harry had been about to deliver.

"Ha-Ree of the Far Star People will stand for the house of all the Sky People in this matter. Grevorg will stand for the Sarmatchani," she proclaimed, both hands raised over her head. It had taken the better part of an hour to explain who Harry and Rodriguez were. The Terran's advanced weapons awed the tribesmen, and constrained by their chief, the clan had offered no direct threat but neither would they yield their claim. The Sarmatchani had grudgingly accepted Harry belonged, in a distant way, to a high-status offshoot of the Zobulakos by virtue of being "from the sky."

"If Ha-Ree should win, the debt by Stabilo is forfeit," Harry heard her say, and jeers from the crowd answered her.

And I get a chance to persuade Daddy, after cutting his kid up in front of him, to start a revolt with me. What a fucking op.

"If Grevorg shall win, the life of Volo will be in his hands," she said, keeping both hands in the air. Cheers rang out, leaving no mistake as to the preferred outcome.

Gotta love a friendly crowd.

Their response gave Harry a reason to scan the people around the circle. As far as he could tell, the men and women wore nearly identical external clothing, rather like the Inuit on Earth. The shaman's shirt was different, overlaid with a vest, upon which was tied a variety of small sachets, bones and dried plants. She pointed to the hill behind them. "When the sun appears above the grass, the fight will begin. It will end when one fighter yields or dies."

"I'm sorry for fight, star-man," Grevorg said, seemingly sincere. Over his shoulder, the sister, not much shorter, glowered wordlessly at Harry as she passed her brother the knife. "Clan law says I must defeat you. If you yield fast, maybe I don't have to hurt you. Much."

The clan version of K'tor was different than what Harry had learned. The differences in pronunciation and slang were manageable, though, and he got the gist of what the fighter was saying. Grevorg was young, and young men were prone to anger. Harry would use that.

"I appreciate the thought, kid," Harry replied a little dismissively. "I'll return the favor."

Grevorg simply narrowed his eyes, stepped forward a pace and settled into a blade-forward fighting stance. Harry reciprocated, but used his lead hand to guard the knife in his right. For several moments they watched each other, motionless, accompanied by the encouraging shouts of the Sarmatchani.

"The sun has arrived," the shaman-woman pronounced.

Like quicksilver, the tall youth immediately struck, trying to score on Harry's empty hand. Harry merely sidestepped, measuring his opponent's speed. Grevorg tried again, extending his arm further, and Harry dodged again, smiling to goad the younger man. He could feel the adrenaline coursing, and he breathed carefully, willing himself to remain calm.

Several of the clan yipped, urging Grevorg on, and his next attack anticipated Harry's sidestep. Harry merely leaned the other way, making the motion seem negligent and casual, causing a few of the watchers to laugh. Harry watched Grevorg grip his knife tightly, squaring fully up with Harry.

He's getting angry. Good. We know what that's like. Yes, we do.

On the next pass, Harry sidestepped, but this time, he used his own forearm to widen the gap and slashed at his opponent's momentarily unguarded flank, scoring a hit. The leather tunic deflected some of the blow, but Grevorg stepped back a pace and dipped a hand to his side, testing the injury. It came away red. He inclined his head to Harry and smiled toothily, while the tribe screeched in excitement. Harry replied in kind, but a wet feeling on his wrist made him glance down. He saw his left sleeve had been opened from wrist to elbow, as neatly as if cut with shears. Underneath, a cut several inches long traced a red line along the thick part of the forearm. He flexed his arm a bit, and the midpoint of the cut gaped like a jeering red smile. Harry hadn't felt more than a sting. Fortunately for him, the cut ran along the grain of the muscle, and function wasn't impaired. Much.

Harry's rage kindled, sending even more adrenaline surging into his system, making him feel preternaturally alert.

Sharp knife and a fast man with more reach. Gotta watch. Gotta think this through.

The two men tested each other's wounds, shuffling inside the circle, searching for openings. Several more quick passes ensued, and Harry acquired three more shallow but productive cuts in exchange for only one deep slash to his opponent's thigh. He reluctantly accepted that his opponent was both faster than him and learning quickly as well. Only minutes in, Harry was breathing like a slow bellows, but Grevorg was panting, growling in anger. Harry continued to fight his own anger down. Anger bred impatience, and he needed the other man to make the first big mistake. For obvious reasons, both men had carefully protected their face and neck during the fight, but if Harry wanted to win this, he had to do so before blood loss became the deciding factor. He needed to render Grevorg helpless and compel a non-lethal end to the fight. They shuffled in a circle, and Harry's shirt grew sodden with blood.

Firearms, not knives, had been the focus of weapons training in the special ops community, but Harry had trained with the Negritos in the Mindanaoan jungle of the Philippine highlands. Their rough and tumble fighting style accepted punishment as the price to close with an opponent. Harry needed to give the kid a target he couldn't pass up. All he needed was a spark.

"I see you've brought your sister along on a war party," Harry said, trying a sneer on for size. "Is that for your convenience or mine, after I win?"

Grevorg fairly roared and sprang towards Harry, who dodged, but feigned a stumble, exposing the upper end and shoulder of his knife arm. The angry youth leapt into the opening and Harry felt excruciating pain along his knife arm and shoulder, nearly making him drop his weapon, but now he had the distance. In a single, fluid motion, Harry drove into pain, feeling the edge of Grevorg's knife drag deeper as he trapped his opponent's wrist and weapon between his shoulder and the man's stomach. He blocked the man's ankle with his own and used his momentum to flip the bigger man off his feet. In a flash, Harry dropped to his knees, one driving deep into Grevorg's abdomen, forcing all breath from his lungs. Harry used his empty hand to deliver a calculated blow to Grevorg's temple, stunning him. Then he placed his own knife against his target's carotid and pressed hard enough to dimple the skin and open a small incision. His hand trembled slightly as the blood sheeting down his numb right arm blended with the fresh cut on Grevorg neck.

Kill him. Do it.

The urge to finish the stroke was strong, but he ignored the raging voice in his head, blinking sweat out of his eyes.

"Yield. Or. Die," Harry panted into the sudden silence, his head swimming.

Grevorg bit his lip but remained mute, shaking his head once. Harry looked up at the shaman and then the chief, struggling to keep his knife steady. He could barely feel his hand now.

"You claimed blood or treasure," he said, glaring at Yannis. "Here is the blood! How much more will you have? We may find it difficult to discuss the future of the Herdbanes if my hands are red with the last of your son's lifeblood."

"Father, n—!" Grevorg's second spat, but their father raised a hand, looking angry enough to chew rocks. He stared at Harry, then at Volo, who was standing mute, watching from the sidelines.

"Raah!" he suddenly yelled, grabbing his braids tightly enough that the muscles of his forearms bunched, his face contorted for a moment in frustration. "Parlay! So be it. First, you need to bind up your wounds before you expire while my clan is in your debt! And someone look to my young idiot!"

He nodded curtly at the shaman, and the circle broke up. A few clansmen as well as Rodriguez and Volo hastened to the combatants. Harry flopped to his side, rolling off Grevorg, and just like that, his rage rolled up, receded out of sight, like a window shade winding back into a hard roll. Grevorg sat up, holding one hand to his neck. They looked at each other, still breathing hard.

"Thank you for my life, Ha-Ree," Grevorg said, waving off his sister who was trying to see to his neck wound, prying at his blood-stained fingers.

Harry meant to nod, but the ground was in the way and his shoulder throbbed with every beat of his heart. He yelled instead as a great weight clamped against his shoulder. He looked over to see Rodriguez leaning on him, hard, both hands on the wound. Blood had already saturated the battle dressing Rodriguez had evidently held at the ready.

"Shit, this is really deep, El-Tee," he said, "Volo—open that second dressing! I can't tell if the artery is cut, and the wound is too high for a tourniquet. We have to pack it, now!"

He looks a little pale. Wonder how much blood I lost. I wonder how bad my arm is.

Harry let Rodriguez work. The pain was bad but seemed very far away. He vaguely felt his body being manipulated this way and that, but presently he felt very tired. Harry didn't notice when the shaman began aiding his teammate, because he was unconscious by then.

* * *

I can make this work! I love you!
I love you, too, but it's too late.
No—it's not too late. I can fix it. I'll come back.
You're gone, my love.
Come back!
It's too late for us, Harry.
No! Noo!

Harry woke up, clutching at the air. Not another hundred years! He fell back right away, breathing hard.

He was on a bedroll combining the synthetic foam pad he'd brought with him and some unfamiliar soft fabric or hide dyed a deep brown. A few candles, tallow by the smell, guttered alongside. Their smoke mingled with a new, astringent scent that filled the concave leather walls surrounding him. His eyes traced the lines of the walls as they tapered to a pointed ceiling a few meters overhead.

Opposite him, Rodriguez had been dozing, but Harry's movement caused him to open his eyes.

"Hello, sunshine," he said, before smacking the heavy skin wall of the tent and shouting, "Hey! Rosha! He's awake."

"How long was I out this time, Marco?" Harry asked, blinking. A small pewter-colored brazier was the source of the bitter smell. It didn't seem to be bothering his faithful NCO.

Another hospital. And more hospital dreams. I hate hospitals.

"All day and most of the next," Rodriguez answered. "You're tore up pretty good. The kid got his knife into your bicep and your delts. Nicked the artery. Bled like a pig and went into shock. I got the antibiotics on it, but you're not going to be good for much for a few weeks and it's gonna be stiff for months."

The flap to the tent was pushed aside and the shaman-woman summoned by the NCO ducked in, her outfit blurring in motion as the assorted decorations and fetishes danced with her movement. She was followed in close order by Grevorg and his sister, Stella. Grevorg had a skin-colored leather patch on his neck, apparently sticking of its own volition. Stella still wore her now-familiar glare.

"You wake at last, Ha-Ree," Rosha said, making her way to his side and sinking onto her haunches. "Welcome back from the dream world. First, I will examine my work. Then you must eat. You lost much blood and need to replace it for your body to heal."

She reached towards Harry's shoulder. Involuntarily, he flinched away and raised one hand. His right hand, on the side gored by Grevorg. Everyone stopped and watched the movement.

"Is there pain?" the shaman asked.

"No," Harry answered, shocked that it was true. He hadn't gotten a great look at the time, but he remembered clearly Rodriguez and Volo working on the wound right next to his face. It had been a massive and deep laceration. He'd seen his own muscle and fascia, clear to the pinkish bone of the humerus.

He shakily moved his arm up and down a little and it began to ache.

"Maybe a little."

"So," the healer said. "Now, we look." She glanced at Rodriguez. "A light, you smelly beast."

"She likes my flashlight better than she likes me," Rodriguez explained, producing a small battery powered Maglite and aiming it down as Rosha moved away the blood-stained padding. "Holy shit! Look at that!"

The wound centered on Harry's upper arm and shoulder was fully closed, demarcated by a bright red, puckered welt, framed by the circle of bright white illumination. He flexed his elbow, and pain, almost like a cramp, bloomed deep in the muscle.

"Good," Rosha said, laying her hand on Harry's arm and gently pushing it down. "Put it down. Now the other arm."

Harry obediently raised his left arm. The deep slashes on the forearms were also closed and were hardly more than red and purple lines. He made a fist and felt a light sting along the skin, similar to what a line of stitches had felt like in the past. Except, there were no stitches. He shoved the blanket down, and the wound on his ribs was similarly closed.

Harry stared in shock, and he could hear Rodriguez's disbelieving mutterings.

"How long has it been?" Harry repeated.

"Nearly two days have you slept," Rosha answered, peering at the wound. She withdrew a little clay pot from a pocket on the belly of her garment and dabbed a finger inside before smearing the line of the incision with a snot-green paste which smelled like a urinal. As she traced the cut, she muttered inaudibly and the touch of her finger grew hot, like a hair dryer left aimed at one's scalp for too long. Rosha continued down every red-seamed wound and then repeated the ritual twice more before settling back on her haunches half an hour later, visibly tired.

"My magic is strong, and as you can see, the wounds are closed and healing."

Harry looked, and sure enough, the redness of the incision lines had faded perceptibly.

"El-Tee, that ain't natural," Rodriguez said in English, staring at impossibly healthy, intact skin. "I've treated every kind of bush injury there is, and I'd have bet my abuela's virtue you'd be screaming in agony without some kind of painkiller. I used the anti-infection stuff we got from the Dornaani, but there's no way the wound is just *gone*."

"Tell you friend not to fear, Ha-Ree," Grevorg said, smiling at the obviously distraught Terrans. "Our shaman is powerful and knows the old ways. See?"

He peeled back the edge of his neck plaster to reveal the shallow cut Harry had inflicted there, and sure enough, it too was barely more than a closed red seam.

"Fool boy, ruining my work!" Rosha said, smacking his hands and carefully resealing the thin leather covering.

"How?" Harry asked in Ktor, not even bothering to conceal his awe. "No disrespect, honored clan-woman, but even our advanced medicines can't accomplish this much, so fast."

"Oh?" Rosha asked, cocking her head. "Truly? The more one uses the old magic, the better it works, and your body responded quite well, as well as our hunters who've used these magics since birth."

She looked at Harry's biggest wound again and sucked her teeth meditatively.

"Perhaps better. I think that apart from scars, there will be no permanent damage."

Rosha peered into the little brazier. She reached down and pulled a little leather sack off her vest. Opening it, she poured a little handful of fine white powder into her palm and weighed it before adding a bit more. Then she tugged a small bunch of dried twigs from the other side of her chest and crumbled one into her palm before up-ending the mixture into whatever was already brewing. Harry realized her decorated vest wasn't the affectation of an indigenous witch doctor: it was a functional combat medic's harness, complete with pharmacy. A fresh puff of smoke and a renewed astringent odor accompanied her actions. "Your body had been drawing on its reserves and now you must eat."

She snapped her fingers.

"Stella!"

The young woman moved up to Harry's bedroll, body-checking her brother out of the way. She held a small, three-legged pot by a handle, its underside charred black.

"Help him sit, you slow oaf," Stella ordered her brother. "He can't eat on his back."

"What's this, Grevorg?" Harry asked, confused as strong hands helped him to sit upright before more blankets and pillows were stuffed behind his back.

"You won the trial," his former opponent said, his tone making it clear that the answer obvious. "When you spared my life, Yannis accepted your offer of parlay. That can't happen till you are well, so we will help you heal. Clan law."

Stella opened the pot and stirred it.

"Open your mouth, Sky Man," she said.

"Use courtesy, sister," Grevorg said. "The law binds Keepers more tightly than others. As you know."

For a moment the siblings scowled at each other, but Stella relented.

"If you please, Ha-Ree," she said, grudgingly. "I help you eat so you heal more speedily."

"Looks like you get to find out if those immunity shots on the station took or not, El-Tee," Rodriguez said with a malicious smile. "Someone had to be first. I'll be over here, just enjoying some of these delicious SpinDog rations."

Harry looked helplessly at the shaman-woman, who stood, hands on hips. She made little urging motions.

"Eat, eat!"

He opened his mouth to protest he could feed himself, and the girl promptly shoved a loaded spoon into it. Harry chewed cautiously. The texture was meaty, and the taste was mildly sweet and salty. As he chewed, he became aware of a growing level of spiciness, like the Thai food served at Sara's favorite restaurant.

"By the way, I saw what they were cooking an' it had at least six legs, if it had a one," Rodriguez offered, gesturing with a plastic spoon.

Despite a pang of homesickness Harry somehow forgot to be mad.

* * *

Volo watched the activity in the camp as it quietly bustled around him. He paid particular attention to the younger women. Even clad in the robes and leathers which protected them from the desert wind, their obvious athleticism was...intriguing. It probably wasn't a good idea, but he couldn't help but imagine some of them wearing the much lighter, form-following station suits worn by the SpinDogs in their off-planet habitat. However, his regard had not been returned, a first for Volo. He'd never lacked for companionship, despite the strictures on sexual relations aboard the *Second Spin*. This was particularly true since even the youngest of the Zobulakos family was still an attractive political match.

However, he'd learned on R'Bak, the same wasn't the case. Despite painful preparation, his musculature and endurance did not compare to that of the natives, or even the Terrans. Oh, he was treated politely enough. The outcome of Tapper's duel had ensured it. But the duel had only been necessary as a result of what was clearly a preplanned maneuver by Volo's idiot brother, Stabilo. The next message Volo had squirted up to the orbiting microsat for relay to *Second Spin* had outlined the situation and the reply from his father contained confirmation.

At least his father would see to Stabilo's embarrassment. Knifing your brother in the back, at least metaphorically, was an accepted ritual during the incessant, internecine struggles for dominance among the SpinDogs. Of course, one was expected to succeed. Failure was gauche, enough so that it reduced one's social desirability. Among the Sarmatchani, allowing a second to stand for you in a duel seemed to have imparted the same taint. And while the duel had extinguished the immediate hostility, the Sarmatchani chief had remained unswayed by Volo's proposals for action against the J'Stull, let alone facing the Kulsians directly, preferring to wait until Tapper had healed.

A movement caught his attention, and Volo followed the headman's daughter with his eyes as she strode into view, lightly stepping between the guy lines along the row of tents, before ducking into the yurtlike structure where Tapper was recovering from the injuries he'd sustained during the duel. The young woman didn't bother to first slap the leather to request entrance, as formal custom required. Volo frowned.

Only two days after the fight, the Terran officer had regained partial use of his arm despite the massive tissue damage and blood loss. Now, he was effectively fully healed, and, unfortunately, the offworlders couldn't stop talking about it. The power of R'Bak's pharmaceuticals was something Volo's father wanted deemphasized in any negotiations with the Lost Soldiers. More important, the Sarmatchani should build a relationship principally with the SpinDogs, not the Terrans, and that wasn't progressing either.

Volo needed something, but he wasn't certain what. In the meantime, he would continue to persuade the clan chieftain, as slowly and subtly as time allowed, that it was in his people's interest to continue to be of assistance.

* * *

After the meal, Rosha and her sidekicks left, promising to return later. Rodriguez had stepped out too, leaving his boss to relax and rest in private. But before Harry could fall asleep, he had a different visitor. A single firm slap on the wall of the tent alerted him even as the flap was swept aside and the gray-maned chieftain swiftly ducked inside. As he straightened, he looked at Harry and raised an eyebrow in restrained greeting before glancing around the space.

"I hate that smell," Yannis said, wrinkling his nose at the vinegary odor wafting from the brazier. "My wife swears it works, but I think she does it just to annoy the young men and encourage them to get out of bed sooner."

"Welcome, honored Yannis," Harry said. The Dornaani language program had emphasized the importance of formal speech, but the taller man made little palm-down motions in response as Harry struggled to sit somewhat more upright. "I wasn't expecting a visit. Please excuse my inability to greet you properly."

"Just woke up after losing half your blood, and still courteous," Harry's visitor observed. "Different from the others we've received from beyond the clouds."

Harry took a few moments to adjust his pillow so he wasn't reclining quite so much. He used the time to give the chief a once over. Yannis has skipped the full cloak he'd worn the morning of the duel. He was also empty-handed when it came to his lance or an obvious gun, though a sheathed knife, similar to the one Grevorg had used, hung on his belt. The man sank easily into a cross-legged position, leaning against the central tent pole.

"Do you receive such visitors often?" Harry said.

"Often enough to see the difference, Ha-Ree," Yannis said. "Rosha has examined you closely, and she confirms what anyone with eyes can see: you are not of the Sky People. Your bones are too heavy. You are too scarred, like a warrior. Your hands are not soft. Your eyes are hot, but you have the *skepsos*, the thinking way of fighting, even when angered. That's how you goaded my son into a loss."

Harry recognized the near-ritual quality of the chief's recitation. This was no casual chitchat and he hadn't the luxury of preparation. The SEAL flogged his mind to full alertness.

"I regret the necessity of wounding Grevorg," he said earnestly. "But, as I explained before the fight, my clan is allied to the Spin-Dogs, the Sky People, because we must create a refuge on this planet while we wait for our comrades to return. And so, we must find allies among your people."

"Grevorg is fine," Yannis waved away the apology. "He learned something valuable. Know that I have spoken to your man, the other star soldier, Rod-ree-gets. He tells me you know of the legends of the Reavers who land on R-Bak as the second star grows close, scorching the land. He says you would fight against those who murder the tribes. He also says you need us. But he doesn't explain *why* you fight."

"They aren't legends, sir," Harry replied. "They're true, and your enemy is already here. Better to fight while you're strong."

"Yes, yes," Yannis said, acknowledging the statement with a wave of one hand. "But what do you get from the fighting? You didn't have to come here."

"We fight so we might have a base, a safe place for our soldiers to rest and ready for another battle," Harry replied. "We fight so the SpinDogs, such as Volo, might have somewhere to land after hundreds of years spent without a planet under their feet."

The smell coming off the brazier was just too strong, and Harry reached over to replace the lid, at least choking off any more of the fumes from deepening the eye-watering atmosphere.

"I know you're brave, Ha-Ree," Yannis said, a small smile playing on his lips. "Only a great hero would dare to change a treatment ordered by the fearsome Rosha. But bravery doesn't explain why you want to fight. Is it just the sting of battle you seek?"

"I've found the 'sting' of battle to be highly over-rated," Harry replied. "I fight when I must."

"Tell me why you must fight for the Sky People, then," Yannis said, looking into Harry's eyes and holding them. "I know what they want. They need land under the suns and our healing plants. They require healthy women who can help them grow their tribe. Most of all, they need allies in order to defeat the Suzerain, his satraps such as the J'Stull, and the beasts who will ravage land. These SpinDogs aren't as strong as the armsmen of my great-grandfather, who wore the colors of the Eastern Hegemon before he fled to become a free man. They aren't as strong as the Suzerain of the North and his army. They have no magic and hope to learn ours. But why do *you*, Ha-Ree, fight? What do you want?"

Harry didn't know whether sharing everything was the smart play or not. What with the blood loss, he wasn't entirely sure he had all of his wits, and besides, keeping track of lies was a pain in the ass. He looked at the little bank of oil lamps which provided inadequate illumination. Tired of the gloom, he lunged halfway out of his pallet and opened the tent flap, letting fresh light—and air—in.

Screw it. The truth it is.

"We want to go home, honored Yannis," Harry replied. "My man and I were stolen not only from our land but from our time by the masters of the Kulsians, whom we call the Ktor. Our families believe us dead. Our country—our tribe—has forgotten our memory and my sons' sons do not know my name. If getting back to our home means helping the SpinDogs, means helping you, means killing every Kulsian on this planet, then we fight."

There was a pause as Yannis digested Harry's reply.

"And how do you propose to help us fight the forces of the Suzerain?" he asked finally. "You are but two, even if you have weapons from the stars. You have no boats, no airships."

The initial orbital surveys had confirmed SpinDog intelligence regarding surface logistics. Harry already knew that as a matter of control, the satraps, including the local J'Stull, largely forbade convoys of ground vehicles, whether mechanized or animal powered.

They did operate lighter-than-air, semi-rigid dirigibles and boats, giving them a tremendous advantage and allowing them to dictate terms to both of their less-well-equipped vassals, as well as any barbarian who decided to contest the balance of power.

"We know the Reavers, as you call them, are already here in small numbers," Harry said. "They, and the Kulsians, are preparing the way for many more. They ready their ground *vehicles*."

He noted Yannis' puzzled squint at the new term. "Wagons and carts which move themselves, equipped with weapons like these, and larger. They can carry more than any ten whinnies and need to be tended by only a few warriors. If we can take them, we deny their use to the Suzerain. The Sarmatchani can use them instead, becoming swift, able to strike in many places quickly, as though you were far greater in numbers."

"Hmm." Yannis was skeptical. "Volo has told us he can ask for help only once from his friends over our heads, and that only if he can report a success. The J'Stull are many and there are many vassals like them. Even a small stone town like Chorat has half a hundred warriors, and again as many militia. And then there are the Reavers, who will have weapons which shoot fire and lightning. You ask much of my people."

"We can teach your fighters new ways of war," Harry answered. "If you can persuade more of your tribes to join us, our numbers will be enough to take the war wagons when we, and not the enemy, choose the time and place of battle. And I ask no more of them than myself."

"I admire your courage, Ha-Ree, and I can see something of your character. Yet you've already lost your clan, as you've said. If you lose here, you forfeit only a hope of seeing your own world. If the Sarmatchani fail in battle, we lose everything."

"One can lose a battle and keep fighting, honored Yannis," Harry countered, leaning forward. "If your clan loses hope, then all is lost. Consider this: Your people understand that the approach of the second sun and the enemies it brings will kill many and drive the survivors from your lands. If the stories are true, and they are, then the Scorching will leave the Sarmatchani to fall so far that your children will struggle for years to regain even as much as you already have. Does my offer of an alliance offer any more danger than that?"

Yannis looked at him and didn't reply for a long time.

Finally, he placed his hands on his knees and said, "How shall we persuade my fellow chiefs to fight when hiding is what has allowed us to survive, so far?"

"What if, instead of having to begin afresh as the second star recedes, your people could begin from where you stand now?" Harry asked in turn, holding up a clenched fist before opening it slowly, as though presenting a gift. "And what if you could shelter as the satraps do? How many more Sarmatchani children would grow to adulthood to serve the clan?"

Harry smiled. "Besides, everyone loves a winner, Yannis. There is a saying among my people, from a warrior-poet who died long before I was born: *'It's loot, loot, loot, that makes the boys stand up and shoot.'* Let us show the Sarmatchani and the other tribes just what winning looks like."

* * * * *

Chapter Five

"Remember, we want them low enough so we can reach them with this," Harry said, patting the shrouded contraption in the whinnie-drawn cart. "But not so low they actually hit you. You're just the decoy."

"I can wiggle better than a Saigon cola girl trying sell you a short-time," Rodriguez answered cheerfully, using English.

"Marco, English or Ktoran. Pick one, not whatever grunting noises you doggies use among yourselves."

"Bait, El-Tee," the noncom replied in Ktoran as he strode to the small group of Sarmatchani waiting for him. He waved a hand over his head in a tight circle, signaling to Grevorg to get a move on. "We'll be the bait the gasbag can't pass up. You just make sure not to miss."

"Hell, I'm an officer, and you *know* what good shots we are!" Harry jibed back, covering his own tension in the time-honored manner.

"Not helping, El-Tee!" Rodriguez threw the last comment over his shoulder as he reached the front of the small decoy group.

There wasn't any more to be said. Harry and the Special Forces sergeant had rehashed the plan each day of their march. The daily message bursts relayed through the satellites had generated replies from Murphy and the planning cell with the SpinDogs. Their critically important updates made the plan possible. There wasn't a lot of room for error. Of course, that wasn't a new factor, not on this op.

Rodriguez had the easier, but clearly more dangerous of the two objectives. In the week since Harry had persuaded Yannis, the tribe had moved higher into the low mountains ringing the desert, drawing closer to the commerce routes used by the satrap's gatherers to trade with Chorat. During breaks in the march and after the evening meal, Rodriguez had trained up a few of the fleetest tribesmen. His decoy group was now armed with all three of the tribe's precious breechloading rifles.

Their projectiles were hand-loaded conical bullets, which were crammed forward into the barrel by the action of closing the breech, and propelled by a limited supply of paper-wrapped black powder cartridges. The nearly prehistoric weapons had been looted during successful skirmishes against the satrap's own bands of hunters. The rifles had limited range and also created a very large cloud of smoke with each shot. Against like opponents, the Sarmatchani employed them no differently than the long bows with which most of the tribe were equipped, which was to say, as part of a general skirmish line. Harry could tell this offended Rodriguez's professional instincts, and the noncom had enthusiastically introduced the basics of coordinated fire and maneuver.

"What does the name he used mean?" Stella asked curiously. She was standing with the rest of the clan, watching the decoy group head toward a convenient gorge. Around them, the land was rock, mostly bare of vegetation. "What is 'el-tee'?"

"It's my rank in our clan," Harry answered. He'd become more accustomed to the local dialect, and now understood some of the vernacular more completely. "I'm a warband leader among my people."

"And you made a death-joke, right?" she asked. "You laugh, but the smile doesn't reach your eyes."

"I did make a small joke, as a way to acknowledge his bravery," Harry explained. "He knows the danger to his group, and he accepts it, so I offered a joke suggesting the danger was even higher. It's a way to acknowledge his bravery without embarrassment."

"Yes, we do much the same thing," Stella said without particular emphasis. "But the danger *is* great. The Kulsian's skyboat is untouchable. My brother's life means much to me and our tribe. My father's honor means even more. If your plan squanders either, you'll answer to me."

Harry knew he should be more used to Stella's casual threats, which were offered pretty much at the end of every other conversation he had with her. With the ease of practice, he dismissed his irritation and focused on the implications of her words. He'd asked the Sarmatchani to extend a huge measure of trust, after all.

The local vassal of the Suzerain patrolled his territory and maintained order using what the tribes considered to be terrifying displays of power. In truth, the technology was no better than what could be found on 19th century Earth. Spectral analysis from the Dornaani suggested the riverboats used wood-, coal-, and kerosene-fired steam engines at an efficiency level barely sufficient enough to buck the strongest river currents. The few semi-dirigibles which patrolled the most important trade routes and borders were limited in payload and speed. However, to a tribe whose movement was entirely limited by how fast they could hike, the Kulsian's technology was awesome, and like the aeroshells which had delivered Harry's team, it represented a magic they couldn't hope to match. All the Sarmatchani clans recognized and resented the impossible advantages conferred by the somewhat common boats and much rarer airships.

Harry knew it, and was counting on it, in fact. En route, the initial band of Sarmatchani had been joined by representatives from neighboring groups. In order to get them to observe Harry's operation at close quarters, Yannis had spent political capital like water, using a mixture of promises of spoils blended with accusations of cowardice. Nearly all had agreed, though they were more cautious than his band, and so would stand off and watch from farther away.

"The skyboat is nothing more than fabric, wood, and a little metal," Harry explained. He'd repeated his explanation every day, but the tribe only followed his instruction because of Yannis' command. "Like you, they think their machines are untouchable. They won't expect our surprise. When they lose their precious gasbag, they'll grow more fearful of the Sarmatchani and your tribe will gain much status."

"I hear your words," Stella said, glancing at him before letting her eyes follow the dwindling figures of the decoy group as they marched toward the lower of the two morning suns. "My lance waits to believe. So, now lead me to the place my father has selected for this folly."

* * *

Harry swept the horizon for the target. Below the rim of the shallow canyon, the decoy group was gathered around a fire, enjoying their afternoon. Harry's first job was simple. The main group would see the airship first, by virtue of their higher vantage point. Then Harry would instruct another to signal those below.

"The breeze is light, as you hoped," Yannis observed, lying next to Harry, covered by a dirt-colored hide which lay across them both, smooth-side up. Harry recognized the blue-black fur from his encounter with the batangs, as the Sarmatchani called the creatures he'd encountered early on. This must have been an even larger specimen whose skin comfortably spanned both men as well as Volo, who lay on Harry's other side.

"*Second Spin* updated the forecast, and winds should remain low," the SpinDog offered. "The message stated the target remains on schedule as of the last satellite pass, a few hours past."

"Thanks, Volo," Harry answered. The satellites had been tracking the surface activity for weeks, even prior to the drop, and the schedule of the boats and airships was consistent. The younger man had seemed content to allow Harry to lead so far. He'd relayed all of their requests for information without complaint and had offered useful ideas which had speeded the construction of the new weapon. "The less wind, the more confident the crew of the dirigible will be," Harry continued.

For a time, they lay quietly, the light breeze rippling along the edge of their covering. Harry left the men to his left and right to their own thoughts. Abruptly, he realized he hadn't thought about Sara for a few days.

Even when she'd been angry with him, Sara would listen to his rants, pick apart his rationalizations, and generally help him be a better person. He'd been so wrapped up in this op he'd not realized how much he missed it.

Get busy, forget your wife. What an asshole I am.

Of course, she always said as long as I was in the field, that's where my head needed to be. Just leave the field behind when you come home.

Home.

Harry tried not to think about home for a while and didn't check his Casio until Yannis bumped his hip.

"There."

Sure enough, the oblong shape of a dirigible was edging around the point, a few klicks away. Harry kicked Volo's ankle, and the SpinDog used a mirror to flash the campfire below, soliciting a flash in response. Invisible to them, Harry knew the decoy team would then use their mirror to "give away" their position to the oncoming airship.

He studied it through his monocular as it grew closer.

The main component was a blunt-nosed fabric cylinder more than a hundred meters long. It was dyed a rust color and tapered from front to back. The semi-rigid vehicle was encased and shaped by a grid of heavy ropes, like a coarse fishing net. Around the midsection or waist of the bag, and integrated into the net, ran what looked like a light gray metal frame, possibly aluminum. The rear of the frame supported control surfaces, built kite-style in a cruciform shape. Dwarfed by the bag, and hanging beneath it, was a long, mostly enclosed gondola with actual portholes lining the sides. It seemed to be at least head-high and from the canoe-shaped stern was hinged a huge wooden-framed, fabric rudder. An exhaust stack projected to starboard, trailing a blue-black haze, presumably from the power plant which was kept well separated from the lift bag above. The motive force was provided by two propellers, whose nacelles were hung from the midships rail. It took Harry a moment to figure out they were running on belt or chain drives leading toward the motor section.

Abruptly, the nose of the ship shifted as the craft changed course, steering directly toward the decoy team.

Excellent. It was time for Rodriguez to wriggle. Right on time, one of the Terran's few ground flares ignited below, the red actinic glare visible even in broad daylight. Nothing in the hands of the tribesmen should burn so brightly, and Harry had calculated the anomaly would draw the craft even closer. Sure enough, it began to descend, approaching the level of the canyon rim where the assault team was hidden.

Harry felt his own excitement build as the parts of his plan came together.

"Yannis, ensure the wagon teams keep the covers on till the last moment," Harry whispered, not taking his eyes off the approaching target. Nothing must give away the ambush until the craft was deep inside his range, even as they thought themselves above the range of bows or captured rifles. It descended a bit more, sinking below the lip of the canyon.

Harry saw the first puff of muzzle smoke from the decoy group as they opened fire. A second and a half later, the sound reached Harry. A second puff, then a third. The airship slowed and began to yaw, and movement was visible inside the control compartment. A few more moments, and a corresponding puff of smoke, though smaller in size, bloomed from the gondola. A much sharper report sounded. Then another and another, until there was an intermittent crackling as the gunners on the ship ruthlessly took advantage of their height.

The gunfight was just like a rock fight in a well, only it was Harry's team on the downside. Only two puffs of smoke replied from the ground.

"Now?" Yannis asked, gripping Harry's elbow. "Now!"

"Not yet," Harry said. He wanted the ship to lose even more momentum so if he missed, he would have time for a second attempt before the craft ascended out of range.

Anxious moments passed, and Yannis' grip grew excruciating.

Good enough. Let's see what Mama Tapper's boy brought to the party.

"*Now!*" Harry shouted, and Yannis stood, throwing off the concealing tarp. Harry remained prone and lowered his head to the comb of his M-14, already laid in front of him. He looked for a porthole which might correspond to the pilot, coxswain, whatever, of the airship. Only two hundred yards away, it was nearly at a dead stop, and even as he acquired his sight picture, he noted the rate of fire from the ship had slowed as lookouts spotted the activity taking place behind Harry. That was a good thing, because the decoy team's fire had dwindled to nothing.

Harry began shooting, punching rifle rounds through the wooden bulkhead of the gondola. Slow, deliberate fire, not faster than one round every two to three seconds. Even without a certain target, his fire would serve to distract the gunners and crew, taking the heat off Rodriguez. After five or six rounds, no more plumes of smoke came from the ship as the rate of enemy fire also dropped to zero, likely in shock. Harry knew his own position would be hard to spot for an enemy accustomed to looking for large blooms of gun smoke. He smiled, imagining the confusion on the airship.

Surprise, motherfuckers. Mr. Murphy would like a word.

Harry couldn't see behind himself, but he knew Yannis and Volo would be exhorting the gunners to get the camouflage covers off the remaining two wagons as fast as they could. He wondered if the torches were lighting from the smoldering tapers they'd had to keep burning all afternoon as they waited. He could hear the clacking as the loaders spun the cranks, drawing back the massive drawstrings of his "surprises." Focused on his shooting, he didn't watch as the improvised Roman-style ballistae, designed and built by the Terrans with considerable and increasingly enthusiastic Sarmatchani wheelwright's assistance, were trained on the target. It had taken nearly as much effort to persuade Yannis to cannibalize half of his clan's wagons for the scheme as it had to attempt the effort in the first place.

Volo had already hustled back to the mechanisms. He was in charge of laying the weapons and alternating fire.

Two ballistae. Why? Because two is one and one is none.

A loud *TUNG!* finally got his attention, and a faint red line arced toward the airship. Amazingly, it tracked true, piercing the bag amidships. Harry waited for a moment, but nothing happened. Both Rodriguez and he had thought hard about the problems of making an incendiary ballista bolt. The SF sergeant, a veteran of myriad booby traps improvised by his Viet Cong enemy, had devised a way to use the burning metal of their red marking flares as a payload that wouldn't be snuffed out by the speed of the ballista bolt. Harry knew—well, believed—the R'Bak satraps were using hydrogen to generate lift. The Dornaani analysis all pointed one way. However, the airship remained intact. In fact, the ship's stack belched a pulse of darker exhaust. Someone was belatedly increasing speed.

I didn't say you could go yet, motherfuckers!

Harry went to rapid fire, using the rest of his magazine to probe the gondola, hoping he was distracting, or better, disabling the crew.

The second bolt fired, also striking the target, but yielding no effect.

They've got to be using hydrogen. There's no way they have enough helium to fill their ships.

He snarled and let a little bit of his bottled frustration and anger out for a glimpse of the world. The bolt locked back on his rifle, so he rocked a new magazine into place and kept firing, this time aiming for the engine nacelles. The airship's acceleration was still building, and the range to target was nearing the limits of their improvised weaponry.

Harry heard a third bolt go downrange, but the unmusical *tung!* was accompanied by a crash and a scream. He looked back to see one gunner facedown and another holding his bleeding arm. The capstan, used to tension the bow, had failed catastrophically, and the parts had been flung in all directions. A materials failure, bad design, the gunners got nervous and over-cranked the machine—it didn't matter. Harry spied Volo at the head of the little crowd staring at the wreckage, and the remaining weapon wasn't in service.

"Volo, make ready to load and fire, goddamit!" Harry yelled. He left the rifle and ran the few meters to the shallow pit that had been used to conceal the wagon-born ballistae. Volo gave him a started look and sprang back into action. Harry snatched the bolt from the Sarmatchani crewman looking askance at the bleeding tribesman on the ground and thrust it at the SpinDog before roughly pushing the chieftain toward the tensioning mechanism. "Yannis, be pissed tomorrow, but spin the crank, now!"

Harry and Yannis worked the alternating handles on the crank, drawing the bowstaves back. Made from the wooden suspension leaves of the cannibalized wagons and inserted into pre-tensioned loops of thick sisal-like plant fiber, they creaked with a strain they'd not been designed to handle. Too much load and they would crack.

Too little and the bolt wouldn't reach the airship, which was now gathering enough speed to respond to the rudder and was already turned all the way to one side. The pawl clacked forward one more time, and Harry stopped.

Volo laid the bolt into groove, ensuring the notch was seated.

"Light!" the SpinDog ordered, and Harry watched as Stella, of all people, laid the torch against the little metal cage immediately behind the spiked business end of the bolt. The mixture of twisted plant fiber, animal fat, and signal flare lit with a sullen red glow. "Training. Stand clear."

Harry itched to aim the weapon himself, but Volo had already achieved two hits. This was their last chance and Volo was the right person.

TUNG!

The group held their breath as the bolt described a graceful arc before curving down and disappearing into the stern of the ship. A moment later there was a sudden glow, and then an audible *whoosh* as a brilliant, glaring light bloomed from the stricken ship. The fire was bright enough to make the daylight seem pale in comparison. Immediately the stern crumpled and sank, arresting the ship's forward motion. The fire ate at the fabric, creeping forward toward the bow. The gondola sagged suddenly, and figures were visible at an open door. A coil of rope spilled out, and a man, then two, grabbed at it and slid down.

Unfortunately, the ship was still much too high, despite the accelerating loss in altitude. The lower man arrested his descent as he reached the end, still fifty meters above the ground. He barely had time to consider the calamity. His fellow didn't stop, and both men pinwheeled, doll-like, from the end of the dangling rope. Their screams lasted only a moment before they disappeared against the dark earth.

A second *whooshing* sound heralded the ignition of the forward gasbag, and Harry put up a hand to shield his face. Even at a distance nearing three hundred meters, the heat was intense, yet thankfully brief. The clan around him was screaming in jubilation, drowning out the distant, thin screams of their unseen victims trapped onboard.

He looked around, an unaccustomed smile slowly growing on his face, as his body rocked from the joyful pounding Yannis was delivering. Stella was screaming a paean of pure triumph and blood. Harry looked at Volo and offered a casual salute, touching two fingers to his brow.

"Good shooting, Volo!" Harry yelled, but he doubted the Spin-Dog could hear him, although he saw Volo grin in response.

Well, maybe there is something to this Lawless thing after all.

* * * * *

Chapter Six

This is even louder than the feast scene from the last Star Wars movie. At least there aren't any of those annoying teddy bears, even if the music is about the same.

Harry gripped his drinking horn tightly as another drunken Sarmatchani slapped him hard enough to bruise, braying his approval and giving Harry a great view of his food-stained mustache, the bristles sticking out at odd angles as the man yelled something congratulatory. Harry just nodded and smiled, since he could barely hear himself think over the sound of the hide drums and buzzing, kazoo-like harmonicas which served the Sarmatchani as musical instruments. He turned carefully, balancing on the three-legged stool propping up his drunken butt, here at the head table. He opened his mouth to address Yannis.

"Well done, boy!" Yannis overrode Harry with a roar, his boozy words accompanied by a bit of spray. "Have I told you how well-done that was!"

Yannis caught sight of something over Harry's shoulder and didn't wait for Harry's answer.

"Excellent, the main course is here for the hero's feast!"

The entire assembled clan had been doing heroic trencher duty for an hour already. Immature whinnie was on the menu, and though it didn't taste just like chicken, Harry enjoyed the spices. Some sort of grain dish, whose individual flat grains were shaped somewhat like pumpkin seeds. More unidentifiable meat, tasting like the first thing Stella had fed him during his recovery. Each place setting had a shallow clay bowl with hot coals and Yannis had shown him how to cook the meat just long enough for it to brown before dunking it in gravy and wolfing it down.

Or doing whatever took the place of a wolf on this damned planet.

He looked for Stella in the crowd below, but he was jostled by two men bearing a wooden tray nearly a meter long. Harry almost recoiled in disgust looking at the contents.

The new dish was a bug. A giant, red and black bug shaped like a lobster, if a lobster had extra legs and the giant hooked mandibles of a mosquito larvae. It was still alive, its segmented body pinned to the wooden tray with sharpened dowels. He swore that the damned thing's eyes were watching him, and the jaws clacked together angrily. Harry could hear Rodriguez groaning next to him.

"Oh shit, I was afraid of something like this."

"Like what, Marco?" Harry said, his voice rising an octave or six.

"That, El-Tee, that's lunch," Rodriguez said soberly. "And you can't flunk lunch."

"What the fuck do you mean?" Harry eased back as the bug tried to escape again. He tried a different tack and addressed the chief. "What the hell, Yannis! What's that?"

"We're lucky, Ha-Ree!" Yannis said happily. "I wasn't sure our hunters could find a nest of *astakos* with so little notice. They are quite rare, but tasty. Their flesh gives a warrior new strength and potency! Haha!"

Yannis dug an elbow in Harry's side hard enough to dislocate a rib, laughing so uproariously that Harry had no doubt what kind of potency Yannis meant. Before he could suggest an alternative to this no-doubt great honor, the drunk chief whipped his belt knife out overhand, severing one of the legs. The creature tried to hunch its back in a pain response, and the armor rubbed against itself at the joints, making a grunching noise while the remaining seven, count 'em, *seven fucking legs*, clattered on the table as it tried fruitlessly to escape.

The chief dropped the spasming leg in his cooking coals, holding it in place with his knife until it stilled. The smell wasn't bad, and the carapace was turning a bright white in the heat.

"Go on, you've earned the second piece!" Yannis prodded Harry. "Only the bravest may sample it! Do watch out for the mandibles, they're quite sharp."

Oh, man. I have to eat a fucking giant cockroach.

He looked over at Rodriguez again, but he was no help. The noncom only nodded sagely, trying and failing to suppress a gleeful smile.

"It's not too bad, El-Tee," he said, motioning to Harry to get a move on before swallowing more of whatever the fermented drink was. "Better than cobra-venom gland sushi, like I had to eat in Cambodia. You gotta eat it, or you're refusing the hospitality of the clan. It would mess up that shiny new hero image you made by shooting down the blimp-thing. This meal is a test. You can't flunk it."

"I didn't shoot it down!" Harry said, looking over at Volo, a couple stools over. "Volo shot it down. He should have the honor!"

Harry glanced down at the struggling bug.

Crunch, crunch.

"On no, Harry—I mean, El-Tee," Volo said, folding his arms and standing. "You're the leader. The honor is yours! No one will be surprised if I, a mere gunner, refuse the honor so a great warrior such as yourself can enjoy this...feast."

I can't believe this shit.

Harry grabbed his horn to swig some of the alcoholic-whatever-it-was and fortify his strength.

"Hey, El-Tee, do you want to know where they get this fermented milk?"

"No. No, I do not."

Harry took a breath, drew his knife, and deliberated which leg he'd choose.

Clatter-clatter-clatter. Gruuuunch.

Just fuck me.

* * *

"Oww," Harry said out loud. He awoke flat on his back, looking up at the ceiling of the same style yurtlike tent as the one in which he'd recovered. He let his memories reassemble themselves in no particular order.

Finding Rodriguez and Grevorg, injured but alive. Searching the crash site for anything valuable. The elated march to a nearby Sarmatchani tribe's village. What else?

Oh right. The traditional Sarmatchani drinking celebration. Fermented...I still don't want to know what it was. And now the traditional penance...

The scent of last night's fire failed to complement the pounding in his head, as he creakily struggled to his elbows. Gray morning light filtered in from the gaps between chimney and the tent roof, and that hurt a bit, too. "Oww."

"Good morning, Ha-Ree."

He started, nearly falling off his short billet, and looked to his right to see Stella. She was under the covers, curled up on her side. Her long, dark hair lay tangled across her bare shoulder. He was suddenly aware of three things. She was gorgeous, he was utterly naked under the blankets, and *holy crap that's the chief's daughter!*

"You've finally awoken," she said, smiling. "I'm glad. You were snoring like a lovestruck whinnie, and I feared lest one hear you and come searching for a mate. Fortunately, I was here to defend your virtue."

"Uhh," was the best Harry could offer. "Thanks?"

"Now you're awake, and I can finally get warm," Stella said happily, scooting under the blankets and draping herself across his chest and other parts. If she was surprised to find him without the approved Sarmatchani pajamas, she gave no sign.

Perhaps the Sarmatchani didn't wear pajamas, Harry thought. *She certainly isn't.*

* * *

An undefinable time later, Harry was still awake, and in much the same position as when he awoke, except this time his head was clear, and his shoulder was decorated with the head of a beautiful woman.

"You demonstrated considerable foresight bringing that jug of water with you," Harry said. After addressing the first round of rather urgent business, Stella had plied him with cup after cup of cool water, and his headache had slowly receded. "Or was it experience? Oww!" he added, involuntarily.

"You think I sneak into tents with drunken strangers as a matter of course, you *skrellig*!" Stella said, her fist cocked back, ready to repeat her punch. "I'm the daughter of—"

"Easy, easy!" Harry wheezed, one hand over his solar plexus. He didn't know what a *skrellig* was, but it probably wasn't a compliment. "I was just asking if you tried that witch's brew we were drinking last night. Maybe you knew that I really needed some water. That's all!"

"Oh," Stella said, suddenly deflating. "I thought that you meant...never mind. Everyone knows that strong drink first brings laughter and then fireside boasting but leaves you with an empty stomach and an emptier head."

She lifted the blanket from his stomach and groin, studying where she'd hit him. "Does it hurt? I don't see a mark."

"No, I'm fine," Harry replied, hastily tugging the blanket back down. "I feel good. Perfect, actually."

"Well, of course you are," she said, matter-of-factly, and rolled away to refill Harry's kidney-shaped canteen cup again from the water jug. "I took some of your anger, so naturally you feel a bit happier. What could be more natural than that?"

"My anger?"

"You hold your anger inside you, like a fist," she said, sipping. "Many could see it. Rosha saw it first. I thought your anger was aimed at us, that you were glad to hurt Grevorg. It's why I didn't trust you. But now we have a great victory, just as you said we would! So, I decided to take some of your anger, to see what's underneath. I should have known."

Harry digested that. About the time he got on active duty, the military was experimenting with psychologists to help operators who had problems. The cost of training a replacement was high enough that it made sense to try to fix the ones they already had. None of his fellow SEALs trusted the concept. Despite having dodged that particular bullet, now Harry was getting his head shrunk by a barbarian girl on an alien planet. It hadn't been what he expected. Maybe if the Teams had beautiful women shrinks, he would have given it a try. Of course, he'd already had a—

"You have a woman," Stella said. It wasn't a question.

"Had," Harry ground out, fighting an intense wash of emotions. Without any warning, his feelings spiraled downwards, like a high-speed canopy malfunction. He attempted to maintain his composure as anger, sorrow, and more anger eroded his failing control. Residual exhaustion, too much drink, and a copious helping of guilt finished him and the anger both, leaving only a surprising emptiness. To his horror, he felt the sting of tears filling his eyes. "She's dead. She's been dead for a long time."

Stella sat up, ignoring any modesty and gently took one of his hands in both of hers.

"Tell me."

So, he did.

He spilled his guts.

What it meant to be in the Teams and how proud he was. How much it cost. His family. Being gone all the time, endlessly deployed. The arguments. The last-moment orders to Somalia, just as he was considering getting out. The absolute wreckage of a country, the lawlessness. The sneering militia who used kids no older than Harry's own sons as cannon fodder, knowing that the soft Americans would hesitate to shoot. The useless UN commanders, padding their careers and lining their own pockets. His decision to make a little justice in a capricious, uncaring universe. How good it had felt, torturing the militia captain who resold the refugees' food, who'd mousetrapped Harry's unit into killing innocents. The consequences. The resulting helo ride. Waking up dead to find himself a century and a half too late to fix anything, after all. All of it.

When he finished he was crying. Big bad, Navy SEAL, leaking all over his own stupid face. Wiping his eyes, he looked at his audience. Stella still held his hand, but she too was crying, tears leaving shining tracks down her cheeks.

"The gods chose you, Ha-Ree," she said with perfect conviction. "I don't know why, or how, but the hand of a greater power is clearly upon you, reaching out to steer your fate."

"Fuck the higher power," he answered vehemently, and then went on somewhat more calmly, gently squeezing her hand. "I didn't ask for this. This moment has been the first decent thing that's happened to me in the last…century."

He laughed as he began his last sentence and then stumbled over the last word as his chuckle nearly turned into a sob. God, he hated being a big wuss. He felt the bedding shift as Stella adjusted something, and he looked up to see her smiling and wiping her eyes.

"So, *this* is the first good thing in your life in so long?" Stella asked, raising one eyebrow, and then the blanket. "And I'm the one responsible? As a warrior-maiden, I find that acceptable. Let's prolong the experience, then."

And she did.

* * *

Volo watched as Tapper emerged from the tent, swinging both arms and stretching. The Terran was followed by Stella. Both appeared to be pretty happy with themselves, and to his surprise, Volo found himself sanguine with the prospect of them pairing off. One of the advantages, in his opinion, of planetside life among the Sarmatchani was the absence of social constraints on relations between men and women, like those imposed by *Second Spin*'s genpop council.

Of course, his mellow feeling was probably influenced by the recent break in his own drought of…activity. Following the successful downing of the J'Stull airship—and his role in the operation—Volo had been propositioned rather directly, and he'd accepted.

His wristcom vibrated as it received the download from the satellite, and Volo retreated to a bit of shade, making it easier to read the shiny display.

He shook his head. It must have been too much to expect that having succeeded against all expectations, their run of good luck was going to hold out. Headquarters was reporting—make that *complaining*. Whatever Volo had done to the J'Stull, it had been overkill. The activity at the Kulsian's clandestine vehicle cache had more than trebled. The equipment, secreted away on the R'Baku surface, was updated and re-used each time planets were at their closest point of approach. With periastron still two years off, the Kulsians should have been working at a languid pace, but now both the cargo vehicles and lightly armored escorts were being fueled and positioned for departure. Volo's little group didn't have weeks longer to plan and execute the convoy seizure mission. They only had days, maybe less.

The SpinDogs might have a real opportunity to interrupt the Cycles which had trapped them off-planet, but it was slipping away, and fast.

A portion of *Second Spin*'s message was doubly encrypted, marked only for his eyes. The victory on the surface, and the consequences, had roiled the SpinDog council. The shifting balance of power now tilted toward the faction that favored using the coming war to "use up" the Terrans, decreasing their numbers and influence. Prior to the destruction of the airship, Volo knew he would have been, at worst, ambivalent about this. However, he was feeling something new, a bond of kinship he'd never before experienced.

Tapper, though arrogant and barbaric, had stood next to him. Moreover, he'd actually trusted Volo to shoot the newly invented weapon, when the entire mission was depending on the gunner's accuracy. Rodriguez, for all his uncouthness and indirect threats, had volunteered to be the highly expendable bait, necessary to lure the ship within range. How many on *Second Spin* would have risked themselves like this?

Who were the old men on the council to dictate to whom Volo should give his loyalty? They weren't here, eating this food and sleeping on the ground! Of course, if Volo did anything but dutifully carry out orders, he would be on his own. He wished he could yank the elders out of their council room and bring them on this march, make them open their eyes.

What was that pungent phrase Rodriguez employed when the Sarmatchani trainees complained, wishing for a chance to rest from his demanding military drills? Ah, yes. *"Shit in one hand and wish in the other, then see which hand fills up first."*

* * *

"What do you mean, the timetable has moved up?" Rodriguez almost yelled and hobbled a step towards Volo before Harry interposed himself. "We're completely out of position!"

Harry noted the attention they were drawing and gestured to his noncom to stand down. Volo had come to them with the latest download from the comm network.

"Ease up, Marco," he asked, rather than ordered. "Let's have a sit-down. Volo, could you repeat that?"

"*Second Spin* relayed that the complete inventory of vehicles has been withdrawn from storage ahead of the worst-case projections," Volo replied, turning to accompany Harry as he led the way along the dirt path to the trestle tables framing the clan's eating and gathering area. Rodriguez and Stella followed, and somehow Rosha attached herself to the little procession. "The number of artificers and technicians is far higher than we thought. Some of the cargo trucks are even being test driven already. We no longer have several weeks. We must move sooner."

"There's no way we can move fast enough to get to the cache before they roll!" Rodriguez almost yelled from the end of the little procession.

"Hail, Yannis," Harry said, spotting the clan chief sitting with some of his men. Harry suspected the burly chief had simply continued drinking into the late morning, but he appeared fresh and rested. The chief roared a greeting, waving a drinking horn made from a hollow tusk nearly half a meter in height.

"Ha-Ree, do all Sky People need so much rest before they can resume toasting our victory?"

"We have received grave word from our friends overhead," Harry replied, sliding onto the stool across from Yannis. "Despite our victory, the J'Stull have crafted a surprise from their defeat. They have accelerated their efforts to prepare the war wagons, the trucks. If we want to capture them for the use of the Sarmatchani, we can't allow the enemy to move the machines to their city."

"Can we simply not melt back into the hills?" Grevorg asked before taking a pull on his own drink using his unbandaged hand. "This we have done before. Let them strike the empty hills and fields with their fist. We will laugh at them from the wastes!"

"We sure can't, battle-brother," Harry answered, shaking his head. He clapped the taller man on his shoulder. "I know it's worked before, but now we have shown them the strength of our hand, and the J'Stull will not forget. If they collect all their war machines, they can follow you much faster than you can run."

"Are these machines like the *ballista* that you made for us to kill the skyship?" Yannis asked pensively.

"No, sir," Rodriguez answered for all of them. "Imagine a wagon made of metal, which doesn't need beasts to draw it, but can move across the ground twice as fast as the fastest sprinter. They'll have guns that can shoot very quickly, like the one the El-Tee used during the fight, but much larger. Each wagon can carry up to ten warriors and all their kit."

Murmurs greeted this description.

"Still, if we run, we may live," a voice called from the circle that had accumulated around the informal council. "Who would want to fight such a machine?"

"None of us have the luxury of running anymore, my R'Baku brothers." Volo, who'd remained standing, stepped forward and faced Yannis. "We've learned something more. The J'Stull and all the satraps are required to keep a high-ranking member of their dynasty on every boat, whether on the river or in the sky. This is their way to ensure all recognize the authority of the vavasors and the vassals, all the way to the Suzerain himself. One such was on the sky boat which we struck down. His death touches the honor of the J'Stull."

"Well, good!" Yannis said happily, and fresh roars answered his declaration. "Tell them to send more by-blows of their so-called royal J'Stull family. We'll simplify the choice their clan head must make among his heirs!"

More roars of approval.

"It won't happen like that, Chief," Harry said, slipping into briefing mode. "Yannis, it *can't* happen like that. The J'Stull can't afford to ignore such a challenge, not if they want to keep their place among the satraps. They are far more concerned with the power of their peers than the threat posed by rabble that is too stupid to live in the cities—I'm sorry, but that's how they think of you. Once they complete their immediate mission—moving the trucks to safety—the J'Stull must settle the account. They must find us and totally destroy the Herdbanes, root and branch, or suffer the same fate themselves at the hand of the Reavers. Even with the new warriors from the other tribes, we don't have enough trained fighters ready to attack a well-protected convoy head-on."

"You're sure, boy?"

"Perfectly sure, Yannis," Harry answered forthrightly. "But we have options."

"Go on, then."

"Chief, the first thing to know about them is that these wagons need three things to work. They work best on roads, and really bad ground will stop them. They have to have fuel, and that fuel is both heavy and easy to burn. And lastly, they have to have trained men to drive and fix them."

Harry stood and tipped over his stool.

"Without all three, their strength is like that of a stool with only two legs."

"And?" Yannis asked. "How do we fight these trucks, these machines of destruction?"

"I don't want to confront them or their escort if I can help it, Yannis, not while they have all three things they need to work," Harry said, reaching to Volo, who placed the plastic-coated map of the region into Harry's hand. Harry opened it and laid it out on the trestle table, moving a few empty plates and mugs to make room. He traced one finger down the road that led to Chorat. "But there is a way to fight the men."

* * * * *

Chapter Seven

"You're getting too close to the head, Ha-Ree," Stella cautioned him, as Harry strode alongside the first whinnie in their column. The Sarmatchani had explained that though the beasts would tolerate a heavy pack saddle and were docile enough to be led, they were dangerously unrideable. "That makes them irritable, and this one will take your arm if you don't move."

Harry looked up at the whinnie. It was mostly tan, though vertical greenish counter shading ran along the rough and creased hide. The great dun beast seemed placid, striding along with the barest serpentine motion. Its colorful neck fringe hung loosely about the long neck, and it didn't look any more agitated than it had at camp, where the Sarmatchani strapped the crates containing a few hundred kilos of improvised charges to its back. None the less, this would be a bad time for one of the explosive-laden whinnies to decide it had had enough. Harry angled his steps to open the distance a bit but maintained the rapid pace that he'd set for the entire task force from the outset.

For a while, only the treading feet of the long column made any noise, apart from the occasional low whistle from a worried or bored whinnie, which was then reassured by a light touch from its handler's goad. Experience had taught Harry that groups would string out during a march, so he looked back over his shoulder to check on the progress of the people behind him. Several Sarmatchani camps had contributed to the force, won over by Yannis' exhortations, and their participation stretched the group out even more. On either side of the road, really not much more than a broad track of rammed earth, rose the grasslands through which Harry had passed much earlier. A curve in the road obscured the back half of the group, though the swaying heads of the whinnies rose above the vegetation, giving the appearance there was a herd of unaccompanied animals passing through.

"I've seen the great bridge," Stella offered after they covered another klick. "It's very big, and very old, older than the Cycles. It's been a part of the land for so long that even the animals make use of it. Do you really think this *demo* you've brought will be enough to damage it?"

"Rodriguez thinks so," Volo announced from his position behind Harry, who was mildly surprised to hear what sounded like genuine admiration in the SpinDog's voice. "And he was right in the matter of the blimp."

"I'm reasonably sure we have enough," Harry answered Stella, working to sound confident. The last thing he needed was second-guessing. "Both Rodriguez and I have a lot of experience. Our modern explosives should enhance the effect of the black powder we've collected from the clans who chose to support us. Plus, I know a thing or two about engineering. If we dig down a bit and bury the explosive, we can tamp the explosion and direct the force. We've got enough people to dig. Easy-peasy, we drop the bridge, and the J'Stull will be trapped on their side of the river until they can repair the bridge. All we have to do is wait for our friends, who will bring many warriors and guns. Then we can force the convoy to surrender."

"I like this plan," Stella replied. "It's simpler than the plan to destroy the airship."

"Simplicity is good," Harry agreed, feeling a bit chuffed by her approval.

"Indeed," Stella replied pertly. "The less time spent on it, the better. No hunting plan goes perfectly. Always, there's a surprise. Why spend so much time on the plan when the warband leader will have to change it?"

"Well, you have to have a plan," Harry answered, automatically stilling the old anger when it made a half-hearted attempt to rise before it was easily quashed by the chuckle that rose in his chest, unbidden, hearing the surety in Stella's voice. "Things don't *have* to go wrong every time."

As they talked, they had approached the crest of latest ridge they had to traverse. Waiting for them was Yannis.

"Take a look, Ha-Ree," he said, holding out the monocular Harry had offered him as a battle-gift. "There's a change."

Harry used bare eyes to stare in the direction indicated by Yannis' finger.

Squinting against the glare, he could make out the bridge, describing a dirty white arc across the darker color of the chasm it spanned. It was closer than the horizon, but still several klicks off. He used the monocular to enhance the view.

"Ah, shit," he said, as his vision cleared. "That is new."

"What's new?" Volo asked, catching up to the trio.

"There's a guardhouse on the end of the bridge. We're going to have to deal with it first. We can't just walk up and plant the charges."

"See?" Stella asked, perhaps a little smugly. "Always the plan changes."

* * *

"All you have to do is get their attention." Harry repeated the instruction to Volo, who was nodding earnestly. "Wait for full dark, then sting them. Get them angry, then run back up the road just fast enough to stay ahead of the reaction force. Do *not* engage with these guys. They outnumber our entire force, and all of them have guns. At some point they'll get tired and break off pursuit, or they'll hear the explosion and turn back. Then you head to the rendezvous."

The young man had insisted on leading one of the three groups Harry had created, and the SEAL officer wasn't spoiled for choice. Harry wished Rodriguez was on hand, but even Rosha's miraculous treatment couldn't restore his leg quickly enough to accompany the forced march, which had lasted a day and a half so far.

The first team had already been dispatched. It included the minimum number of Sarmatchani required to keep the whinnies calm and be ready to lead them to the bridge with the explosives. Hidden behind a hill, they would stay well back until Harry called them in by runner. Harry had asked Yannis to stay with the mixed crew of Sarmatchani. The towering chieftain's presence would be more than enough to enforce discipline among the clansmen, ensuring that they didn't move prematurely and compromise the operation. Now that they were nearly at their destination, the big lizard-like animals actually *were* becoming restless, as though they could sense the impending action.

The second group was led by Volo. He would be responsible for the largest number of Sarmatchani, who had to stage a noisy demonstration against the force guarding the bridge. Then, they had to *appear* to flee, encouraging pursuit. Harry just hoped that the kid would keep his head. Volo needed to retreat in time to allow the Sarmatchani with him to not only serve as tantalizing bait, but actually remain outside the reach of the reinforced company of J'Stull who'd materialized at the vital bridge.

The third group was the smallest, led by Harry. It would sweep the bridge of any residual guards and call in the whinnies. Harry would lead the diggers and expose as much of the two key trestles as possible before burying the explosives and lighting the fuse.

"No problem, El-Tee," Volo said, slapping Harry's shoulder. "We'll make beaucoup demonstration, and Mr. Charles will chase our pretty asses all the way home!"

"Kid, you've been spending *way* too much time with Rodriguez." Harry wryly shook his head, before gripping the SpinDog's hand for a quick shake. "You don't want to end up like him. Good luck, and watch your ass."

Volo flashed him a quick smile and trotted back to his command, rapping out orders in a low voice. Harry watched the thirty Sarmatchani melt into the dusk, already shaking out into skirmish order as they disappeared into the grass. He looked at the eight men he'd kept to sweep the hopefully empty guardhouse. All right, six men, two boys who could run like hell, and one very determined woman. Harry had picked the kids because he needed someone to get word to the explosives team. Stella had picked herself, appropriating her injured brother's rifle, but wearing her own knife. All of them wore their hunting leathers and had shovels or spades slung rifle-fashion.

They'd kept their lances to hand and had dulled the shine of their faces with ashes.

"We wait for the shooting to die down and swing in behind the J'Stull," Harry reminded them. "Then we clear the shack on our side of the bridge and four of us dig like hell while the rest pull security. As soon as the holes are halfway, the two runners carry the word to Yannis. He brings in the explosives, then we backfill and boom! Got it?"

Harry looked around the little circle, receiving nods from each man and, for once, a serious look from Stella.

"All right, let's settle in and wait. Stay close enough to touch the man to your right. When you feel the tapping, pass it on and be ready to go."

His team briefly milled about before finding a spot for the wait. Sitting down, Harry couldn't see any further than the person next to him. Stella was sticking close. The group quieted down as the night sounds resumed around them. Harry knew that they had at least an hour before Volo would start anything, and then another ten minutes or more before the commander of the bridge security company decided to do something about it. If Harry had learned anything in the Teams, it was to take advantage of small moments like this, so he tilted his head back and looked at the stars.

Here he was on another battlefield, hell, another planet. So much for getting out of the Teams. In a little while, he was going to lead a mostly untrained assault team on a night demolition assault. Good thing night operations were simple and *never* went wrong. By way of an unexpected twist, he was taking a woman with him. At least that was a first. He looked over at the dark shape of the woman next to him. Of course, Stella wasn't your average girlfriend. Like the rest of the warriors, she'd simply settled in, waiting quietly.

No chitchat, no last-minute fidgeting.
I wonder what she thinks about us?
Us? Is this a relationship?
Man, this is the weirdest pre-mission pep talk I've ever given myself. Time to get the game-face on.

Harry mentally shook himself, and then rehearsed all the steps needed to close the distance to the gatehouse and clear it. He was checking off the list for the umpteenth time when the crack of rifle fire seized his attention.

"Volo's getting started," Stella whispered.

"No need to whisper," Harry said in a more normal tone of voice. "No one is going to hear us over the sound of that."

"That" was an impressive fusillade. Harry knew Volo's group didn't have many firearms, so the J'Stull security company was as heavily armed as Harry had feared. There was a brief *whooshing* sound and Harry grinned. The kid was doing all right. Harry had shown the Sarmatchani how to make black powder bottle rockets and Volo was using several of the things to create even more noise and confusion. The J'Stull would be surprised since they'd never encountered their like before.

"What's going on?" Stella asked.

"Volo's doing his job," Harry answered. "Don't worry. It's all sounds good, so far."

The rockets were simple noisemakers, but their mere presence increased the pressure on the commander to do *something*. At least, that was the plan. A loud horn was sounding from the bridge now and the gunfire from the road sounded like only a few rifles remained, using slow fire. Good. Volo had probably pulled part of his force a short distance back so the front line could simply turn and run under the cover of the first group's fire. Rodriguez had done a good job training the kid.

The horns sounded again, and this time Harry could hear harsh yells, unmistakably the sounds of leaders marshaling their men in the dark, getting ready to chase the irritating Sarmatchani.

A few more rifles cracked, and there was a brief silence. Harry could actually make out some of the shouted commands.

"Close up! Close up!"

"Let's get those shiteaters!"

Then the Sarmatchani's deeper, booming fire picked up again, just enough to goad the J'Stull into accelerating their pursuit, trying to close the distance to these savages that dared to attack them on the J'Stull's own ground. Harry could make out the jingle of equipment as small units trotted past on the road to his side. The rifle fire sounded further away and still he sat, waiting.

After his Casio showed the ten-minute mark, he tapped Stella on the arm.

"All right, brothers," he said, standing, "let's go bag a bridge."

* * *

The good news was that the J'Stull left behind were neither especially numerous nor skilled. Harry's group had approached quietly and fallen upon them with the fury known only by those who've killed with cold steel. Harry led the assault, padding down the track toward the yellow glow of the guardhouse windows. The external guard had been standing at the edge of the area cleared of the tall grass, twenty meters from the adobe building. Unfortunately for the sentry, he was looking back at the building he was supposed to guard. At the last second, he jerked his head up, perhaps finally hearing the tread of the assault group or the sound of their passage through the dense foliage.

He was the first to die, dropped with a single round. Harry used the follow up shots from his M-14 to hollow out the cluster of organized defenders rushing out of the building, while the howling Sarmatchani swarmed, spears forward. The six J'Stull survivors had the presence of mind to return fire but the nomads screaming out of the darkness made for poor targets. Only one tribesman died and three more, including one runner, were seriously injured. In moments, all twelve defenders were cut down and Harry quickly organized the bloody aftermath. He ignored the bodies of the enemy, but adrenaline-fueled rage tingled in every extremity as he contemplated the death of men who had been his teammates. Instead of yielding to his anger, he organized the remaining Sarmatchani who were gaping at the electric light, rudimentary radio, and the firearms laying there, *just for the taking.*

Harry led them and the surviving runner topside before he and the diggers scrambled down the steep bridge abutment, seeking the first upright pier. It loomed in the darkness, cool to the touch. The pier was rectangular in cross section and a meter thick. Harry quickly organized two of the Sarmatchani to dig on the uphill side while he, the last clansman, and Stella searched for the next pier. Ears ringing, Harry could barely hear the sound of his spade biting the dirt, but his battle adrenaline fueled his efforts. For once his anger served a good purpose. As soon as the hole was knee-deep, he turned to order the last Sarmatchani to dispatch the runner while he and Stella finished digging.

Before he could get the words out, fresh gunfire shook the narrow canyon.

"The fuck is that?" Harry yelled at no one in particular.

He exchanged a shocked look with the man he'd been about to address. All three fought their way back up the steep abutment, swearing at the loose, treacherous footing. Above their heads, more fire was being exchanged, and Harry readied his weapon to the sound of screaming.

The Sarmatchani cleared ground level first, just ahead of Harry panting in second place. A heavy caliber bullet tore through the man's head, painting Harry with a hot spray of blood. Ahead of the fresh corpse lay the cooling bodies of the other diggers. Harry dove to one side, rifle up, searching for targets.

There were plenty. Fully another half-dozen J'Stull soldiers were in view, spanning the clearing which faced the end of the bridge. They were still firing into the guardhouse where Harry'd left the survivors of his first attack. There was no return fire. Harry rolled sideways and down, seeking the concealment of the tall grass at the lip of the canyon. Leopard crawling along, he heard a couple rounds rip through the grass waving over his head in response to his passage. He needed to move even faster, so he rose to get a look and bounded forward, using the age-old mantra of the combat infantryman.

I'm up, he sees me, I'm down.

Just in time, because about half the J'Stull fired at his momentarily visible shape. Harry moved a few meters laterally, and then popped up to return the favor, hitting one J'Stull high on the shoulder and spinning him down to the grass. Harry looked for Stella, but she wasn't visible. He'd last seen her on the final climb up the slope.

Had she assaulted forward without him? He peeked but didn't see her body.

Where is she?

He fingered his only fragmentation grenade, brought all the way from Earth. Between his superior rate of fire, and the little olive drab sphere, he had a chance. First, he needed the enemy to bunch up. He'd have to make sure he didn't hi—

"Skyman!" an unfamiliar male voice cried out. "Skyman, I know you are there!"

Harry jerked so hard he popped his neck.

"Skyman! I have your woman!"

What the hell? Are you fucking kidding me?

Harry moved very slowly to the edge of guardhouse. The view stopped his heart. A very tall man, as tall and as broad as Yannis and a J'Stull officer by the richness of his uniform, stood just outside the circle of yellow light cast by the surviving electric lights in the guardhouse. He was clearly daring anyone to chance a shot. He could afford to because he had a firm grip on Stella's bloody right arm. Harry quickly scanned around, spotting two hidden guards who'd stayed further back in the grass, but the bulk of the enemy were arranged around their commander. They must have attacked across the bridge and chased some of the Sarmatchani back into the brush before turning around to spot the dig team.

Harry's anger bloomed anew. His woman, his team. His mission. He began to breathe deeply, fully, adding oxygen to the fire of his rage.

Harry looked back at Stella. She was bleeding heavily from her arm and shoulder and though her face was tilted forward, partially obscured by her hair, he could see blood there, too. Where had this asshole come from? Harry's stomach fell when he realized there must be two guardhouses. He'd missed the second one from a distance, and by the time they were close enough, the light had already begun to fail. This force would've been a couple hundred yards away, across the causeway. It had taken them this long to decide to move over, likely because they hadn't been able to raise friendly forces on Harry's side.

"Skyman! I know who you are! I know about your plan to shame the J'Stull, to attack the property of Kulsis, rightful overlords of R'Bak. Surrender, and I'll spare this bitch."

This guy was way too well informed. Harry and his anger wanted time, more time, ask me for anything but time, but this fucker was going to shoot Stella. Harry desperately flogged his brain for any combination of tactics and weapons that could turn this around. He might be able to drop the commander, but it wasn't a sure thing, since he was shooting over open sights at night at a moving target. But then Stella would die at the hands of the others. If he used the grenade, he'd probably frag himself. It would kill Stella, for certain.

Dying wouldn't be so bad, his anger whispered.

"Let her go, and you can have your bridge!" Harry yelled from behind the adobe wall, staying deep in the shadows. He saw gun muzzles snap in his direction and then weave, looking for a definite target. He mastered his rage one more time. "I'll leave this place."

"You'd give me what I already have?" the officer said, sneering. "How generous. Perhaps your woman can convince you."

With that, he dug a finger into the wound on Stella's arm, and she screamed, high and breathless, hanging from her captor's iron grip.

"No!"

Harry didn't even think, he stood and drew a perfect bead on the man's face. Before he let this bastard hurt her again, he'd drop the man, consequences be damned. He began slowly pacing forward, heel-and-toe, carefully maintaining a sight picture. The front sight was razor sharp, his target a bit blurry and the night-blanketed grasslands behind were just a dark blur.

"Let her go or die, asshole."

"Careful, hero," the J'Stull soldier said, giving his limp captive a shake.

Harry stopped a few paces away. He could see Stella better now. She raised one hand to sweep her hair aside, revealing her unexpectedly composed features and as he watched, her eyes slitted as she evaluated their predicament.

Harry checked the position of the two snipers, but one was missing. While he watched, the second was yanked sideways, snagged by an invisible, irresistible force whisking him out of sight and deeper into the grass. A dull *thud* and grunt punctuated movement.

"Sir, sir! Behind us!" cried one of the J'Stull.

"Call them off or she dies!" the officer yelled, shaking Stella like a terrier shakes a rat.

Harry could see the source of the motion now. Hulking blue-black forms were ghosting forward, staying outside the circle of illumination. Harry lowered his rifle to the ground, slowly, slowly, and kneeled. His rage howled, but Harry shoved it down, down deep, and reached for their only chance.

"Harry, no!" Stella cried.

"Baby, just be quiet and relax," Harry said, his voice low and urgent.

The J'Stull officer was clearly puzzled, looking left and right for his missing men, but he kept the gloating smile on his face as he surveyed his kneeling enemy.

"Fool. Your life is mine n—"

And the first batang bounded into the clearing, smashing into the nearest soldier. It hooted like a base trumpet as it knocked him down, and then grabbed his arm and neck as the soldier thrashed, trying to escape. The burly animal straightened its arms, like a washer woman spreading laundry on a line, and detached the man's limb before discarding his victim on the ground.

Hoots and whistles came from every side as dozens of the creatures, including a particularly huge specimen, shuffled quickly into view. Shots rang out and some batangs screamed, sounding like steam whistles. Harry lay flat, arms at his side, watching as the officer released Stella and raised his own weapon. Another hairy form plowed into him, driving the man into the grass as Stella slumped motionless to the ground. The officer disappeared from view. Then his head bounced back into the clearing.

In moments, no men were left standing, and the clearing was full of grunting, hooting, and agitated batangs, slapping the ground. A few would dash up to a warm corpse and strike it before dashing away again. The largest batang, a huge monster that towered nearly three meters tall, shuffled forward, snuffling from its nasal slits.

Harry held very still as the batang drew within touching distance. It stamped the ground, and snorted. The rest of the troupe grew quiet. Harry remembered Volo's words, and kept his eyes down, staring at the horny, spiked digits that tipped forearms many times thicker than his own legs. A procession of animals moved past, seemingly endless but in reality only taking a minute or two. Slowly, almost ponderously, the largest batang moved off. After another moment, Harry turned his head to see the tall animal shuffle-walk onto the bridge and disappear into the darkness, going about the important business of migrating, and leaving human business to the humans.

Around him lay bodies and parts of bodies, but heedless of the gore he scrambled over to Stella, who was curled into a tight fetal ball. As he approached, she looked up and then lurched to her knees to embrace him.

From out of the darkness, a final hooting call echoed across the canyon.

* * *

"Are you sure you're supposed to be standing?" Harry asked, carefully holding his arm around Stella without actually resting his full weight on her. This was the first that he'd seen Stella up since she got shot. "Rosha seemed quite specific you were to rest. Most of what comes next is just waiting, anyway."

"It isn't every day of my life that I get to see, what did you call it, an *assault shuttle*, land next to my camp," Stella retorted, reaching up and tugging his arm more fully onto her shoulders. "The bones have knit and the holes from the bullets are closed. I can even move the arm as long as I'm careful."

"That arm is staying in the sling," Harry insisted.

A double *crack* sounded across the sky, causing two rabbit-sized creatures with long legs and tails to take flight, their membranous wings pumping furiously.

"Ah, Ha-Ree, your friends come now, yes?" Yannis said, ambling over and scratching the hairy stomach peeking from behind his vest. "Soon we attack the J'Stull city?"

"Yeah, that's them, honored Yannis," Harry replied, looking upwards for the tell-tale contrail. Once the bridge had been blown, Harry had uploaded the sitrep on the next satellite pass, and Volo had received it even before they'd met at the rendezvous. Overhead imagery had confirmed that two full spans had failed on the ancient, inexplicable structure, trapping the J'Stull convoy. "Soon you'll meet my comrades and we will take the war to Chorat, and then across the face of R'Bak, itself."

Stella slipped free her arm around Harry's waist, a motion detected by Yannis. The chief concealed a smile behind a cough, and clapped Harry on the shoulder, though much more gently than he'd ever done before.

"We will have a tremendous victory feast tomorrow, Ha-Ree!" Yannis exulted. "We will drink to the death of all J'Stull and their works! Your friends will attend!"

It wasn't a suggestion. Harry winced internally, wondering how he was going to introduce the mixed bagged of rugged individualists from old Earth to this nomadic chieftain. Then again, he'd like to see Major Murphy deal with it. It wasn't his problem, anymore.

And that's worth a smile.

"How did you know about the batangs, Ha-Ree?" she asked, reclaiming Harry's attention.

"I didn't." He glanced at Yannis just as the older man hid a crafty smile, looking away. "But I'm pretty sure your father did. Probably why he was so confident. How the heck did he—?"

"It was Rosha who summoned them and marked Father as an alpha. But I was not asking how you knew the batang were paralleling us; clearly, you did not. I mean, how did you know how to react when they appeared? Batang are particularly dangerous when they are traveling with young. Yet you knew to neither flee nor fight. How?"

"Volo warned us early in our trip," Harry replied. "He insisted that we remain calm and let the batangs pass. It worked the first time, so…"

"I could see that you were ready to loose your anger," Stella said firmly. "I was angry you might sacrifice the quest just because that *skrellig* gave me a small hurt."

"There she is!" whooped Rodriguez from atop one of the clan's wagons. "Hell yeah, bring me that dust-off, boys! I got me a ride on the freedom bird!"

Harry looked, and high up in the brilliant blue sky, he saw the contrail left by the shuttle, describing arcs across the sky as it turned, bleeding off excess speed.

"I will never again trade your blood for anything," Harry said, looking back at Stella. He watched her eyes widen fractionally. "No hurt to you is a small hurt, my love."

"So, I'm your love now?" she answered, smiling broadly, even joyfully. "You will give me all of your anger? You will be my mate?"

Holy crap, she's proposing to me!

Harry heard the crowd murmur, so he looked up again. The tiny cruciform shape of the dropship was barely distinguishable, drawing the long white line behind it as if by magic.

"Yes," he said, still looking at the ship. He looked back down at his woman and slipped his arm from around her shoulders to face her fully and take both of her hands in his. "Yes. And you'll be mine."

He noted in passing he was trembling like a racehorse before the gate. Big bad Navy SEAL was as nervous as a virgin.

Damn. I've heard of getting the shakes during a drop, but this is ridiculous.

* * * * *

ABOUT THE AUTHOR

Mike Massa writes Science Fiction, Military SF, Fantasy and Post-Apocalyptic Fiction, in addition to non-fiction articles for publication. His most recent novel, co-written with John Ringo, is national bestseller River of Night (2019), book six in the NYT best selling Black Tide Rising series. Since 2016, he has written two novels, a novella and a dozen short pieces which have been included in as many anthologies. He currently works for an award-winning research university, integrating machine learning and artificial intelligence technologies into practical applications for logistics, predictive maintenance, and cyber-defense. Or, you know, Skynet. Whichever comes first.

Before he began writing, Mike lived an adventurous life, including stints as a Naval Officer (1130), an investment banker, a security and anti-fraud expert, and a tech entrepreneur. He has lived outside the US for several years, plus the usual military deployments. Mike is married and enjoys the challenges of three sons and a growing cohort of grandsons all of whom check daily to see if today is the day they can pull down the old lion. Not yet...

* * * * *

The Caine Riordan Universe

The Caine Riordan series and Terran Republic universe deliver gritty yet doggedly optimistic hard scifi in a world that is a believable and embattled successor to our own. For those who are not familiar with the series' hallmark blend of exploration, alien encounters, intrigue, and action, you can find them all right here:

The **Caine Riordan** series
(Baen Books)

Fire with Fire
Trial by Fire
Raising Caine
Caine's Mutiny
Marque of Caine
Endangered Species (forthcoming)
Protected Species (forthcoming)
Triage (forthcoming, with Eric Flint)

The **Murphy's Lawless** series

Shakes
Obligations (coming April 20, 2020)

Other works in the **Terran Republic** universe

Lost Signals (Ring of Fire Press)

Since that list includes a winner of the Compton Crook Award, four Nebula finalists, and two Dragon finalists, they're not hard to find. Just go wherever books are sold. Want to learn more about the Caine Riordan series? Easy. Contact any of the publishers, or you can reach out to me at contact@charlesegannon.com.

Want to see more of what's going on in the Terran Republic universe? Check out http://www.charlesegannon.com for exclusive written and visual content.

And if you decide you don't want to miss a single new release or announcement, then go to http://charlesegannon.com/wp/sign-up/ to join the all-inclusive mailing list for sneak peeks, special offers, and features you won't see anywhere else.

And most important of all...welcome aboard; we're glad you're here!

The following is an
Excerpt from Book One of the Revelations Cycle:

Cartwright's Cavaliers

Mark Wandrey

Available Now from Seventh Seal Press

eBook, Paperback, and Audio Book

Excerpt from "Cartwight's Cavaliers:"

The last two operational tanks were trapped on their chosen path. Faced with destroyed vehicles front and back, they cut sideways to the edge of the dry river bed they'd been moving along and found several large boulders to maneuver around that allowed them to present a hull-down defensive position. Their troopers rallied on that position. It was starting to look like they'd dig in when Phoenix 1 screamed over and strafed them with dual streams of railgun rounds. A split second later, Phoenix 2 followed on a parallel path. Jim was just cheering the air attack when he saw it. The sixth damned tank, and it was a heavy.

"I got that last tank," Jim said over the command net.

"Observe and stand by," Murdock said.

"We'll have these in hand shortly," Buddha agreed, his transmission interspersed with the thudding of his CASPer firing its magnet accelerator. "We can be there in a few minutes."

Jim examined his battlespace. The tank was massive. It had to be one of the fusion-powered beasts he'd read about. Which meant shields and energy weapons. It was heading down the same gap the APC had taken, so it was heading toward Second Squad, and fast.

"Shit," he said.

"Jim," Hargrave said, "we're in position. What are you doing?"

"Leading," Jim said as he jumped out from the rock wall.

* * * * *

Get "Cartwright's Cavaliers" now at:
https://www.amazon.com/dp/B01MRZKM95

Find out more about Mark Wandrey and the Four Horsemen Universe at:

https://chriskennedypublishing.com/the-four-horsemen-books/

* * * * *

The following is an
Excerpt from Book One of the Salvage Title Trilogy:

Salvage Title

Kevin Steverson

Available Now from Theogony Books

eBook, Paperback, and Audio Book

Excerpt from "Salvage Title:"

The first thing Clip did was get power to the door and the access panel. Two of his power cells did the trick once he had them wired to the container. He then pulled out his slate and connected it. It lit up, and his fingers flew across it. It took him a few minutes to establish a link, then he programmed it to search for the combination to the access panel.

"Is it from a human ship?" Harmon asked, curious.

"I don't think so, but it doesn't matter; ones and zeros are still ones and zeros when it comes to computers. It's universal. I mean, there are some things you have to know to get other races' computers to run right, but it's not that hard," Clip said.

Harmon shook his head. *Riiighht,* he thought. He knew better. Clip's intelligence test results were completely off the charts. Clip opted to go to work at Rinto's right after secondary school because there was nothing for him to learn at the colleges and universities on either Tretra or Joth. He could have received academic scholarships for advanced degrees on a number of nearby systems. He could have even gone all the way to Earth and attended the University of Georgia if he wanted. The problem was getting there. The schools would have provided free tuition if he could just have paid to get there.

Secondary school had been rough on Clip. He was a small guy that made excellent grades without trying. It would have been worse if Harmon hadn't let everyone know that Clip was his brother. They lived in the same foster center, so it was mostly true. The first day of school, Harmon had laid down the law—if you messed with Clip, you messed up.

At the age of fourteen, he beat three seniors senseless for attempting to put Clip in a trash container. One of them was a Yalteen, a member of a race of large humanoids from two systems over. It wasn't a fair fight—they should have brought more people with them. Harmon hated bullies.

After the suspension ended, the school's Warball coach came to see him. He started that season as a freshman and worked on using it to earn a scholarship to the academy. By the time he graduated, he was six feet two inches with two hundred and twenty pounds of muscle. He got the scholarship and a shot at going into space. It was the longest time he'd ever spent away from his foster brother, but he couldn't turn it down.

Clip stayed on Joth and went to work for Rinto. He figured it was a job that would get him access to all kinds of technical stuff, servos, motors, and maybe even some alien computers. The first week he was there, he tweaked the equipment and increased the plant's recycled steel production by 12 percent. Rinto was eternally grateful, as it put him solidly into the profit column instead of toeing the line between profit and loss. When Harmon came back to the planet after the academy, Rinto hired him on the spot on Clip's recommendation. After he saw Harmon operate the grappler and got to know him, he was glad he did.

A steady beeping brought Harmon back to the present. Clip's program had succeeded in unlocking the container. "Right on!" Clip exclaimed. He was always using expressions hundreds or more years out of style. "Let's see what we have; I hope this one isn't empty, too." Last month they'd come across a smaller vault, but it had been empty.

Harmon stepped up and wedged his hands into the small opening the door had made when it disengaged the locks. There wasn't enough power in the small cells Clip used to open it any further. He put his weight into it, and the door opened enough for them to get inside. Before they went in, Harmon placed a piece of pipe in the doorway so it couldn't close and lock on them, baking them alive before anyone realized they were missing.

Daylight shone in through the doorway, and they both froze in place; the weapons vault was full.

* * * * *

Get "Salvage Title" now at: https://www.amazon.com/dp/B07H8Q3HBV.

Find out more about Kevin Steverson and "Salvage Title" at: http://chriskennedypublishing.com/.

* * * * *

The following is an
Excerpt from Book One of The Progenitors' War:

A Gulf in Time

Chris Kennedy

Available from Theogony Books

eBook, Paperback, and (Soon) Audio

Excerpt from "A Gulf in Time:"

"Thank you for calling us," the figure on the front view screen said, his pupil-less eyes glowing bright yellow beneath his eight-inch horns. Generally humanoid, the creature was blood red and had a mouthful of pointed teeth that were visible when he smiled. Giant bat wings alternately spread and folded behind him; his pointed tail could be seen flicking back and forth when the wings were folded. "We accept your offer to be our slaves for now and all eternity."

"Get us out of here, helm!" Captain Sheppard ordered. "Flank speed to the stargate!"

"Sorry, sir, my console is dead," the helmsman replied.

"Can you jump us to the Jinn Universe?"

"No, sir, that's dead too."

"Engineer, do we have our shields?"

"No, sir, they're down, and my console's dead, too."

"OSO? DSO? Status?"

"My console's dead," the Offensive Systems Officer replied.

"Mine, too," the Defensive Systems Officer noted.

The figure on the view screen laughed. "I do *so* love the way new minions scamper about, trying to avoid the unavoidable."

"There's been a mistake," Captain Sheppard said. "We didn't intend to call you or become your minions."

"It does not matter whether you *intended* to or not," the creature said. "You passed the test and are obviously strong enough to function as our messengers."

"What do you mean, 'to function as your messengers?'"

"It is past time for this galaxy's harvest. You will go to all the civilizations and prepare them for the cull."

"I'm not sure I like the sound of that. What is this 'cull?'"

"We require your life force in order to survive. Each civilization will be required to provide 98.2% of its life force. The remaining 1.8% will be used to reseed their planets."

"And you expect us to take this message to all the civilized planets in this galaxy?"

"That is correct. Why else would we have left the stargates for you to use to travel between the stars?"

"What if a civilization doesn't want to participate in this cull?"

"Then they will be obliterated. Most will choose to save 1.8% of their population, rather than none, especially once you make an example or two of the civilizations who refuse."

"And if *we* refuse?"

"Then your society will be the first example."

"I can't make this kind of decision," Captain Sheppard said, stalling. "I'll have to discuss it with my superiors."

"Unacceptable. You must give me an answer now. Kneel before us or perish; those are your choices."

"I can't," Captain Sheppard said, his voice full of anguish.

"Who called us by completing the quest?" the creature asked. "That person must decide."

"I pushed the button," Lieutenant Commander Hobbs replied, "but I can't commit my race to this any more than Captain Sheppard can."

"That is all right," the creature said. "Sometimes it is best to have an example from the start." He looked off screen. "Destroy them."

"Captain Sheppard, there are energy weapons warming up on the other ship," Steropes said.

"DSO, now would be a good time for those shields…" Captain Sheppard said.

"I'm sorry, sir; my console is still dead."

"They're firing!" Steropes called.

The enemy ship fired, but the *Vella Gulf*'s shields snapped on, absorbing the volley.

"Nice job, DSO!" Captain Sheppard exclaimed.

"I didn't do it, sir!" the DSO cried. "They just came on."

"Well, if you didn't do it, who did?" Captain Sheppard asked.

"I don't know!" the DSO exclaimed. "All I know is we can't take another volley like that, sir; the first round completely maxed out our shields. One more, and they're going to fail!"

"I...activated...the shields," Solomon, the ship's artificial intelligence, said. The voice of the AI sounded strained. "Am fighting...intruder..." the AI's voice fluctuated between male and female. "Losing...system...integrity...krelbet gelched."

"Krelbet gelched?" the DSO asked.

"It means 'systems failing' in the language of the Eldive," Steropes said.

"The enemy is firing again," the DSO said. "We're hit! Shields are down."

"I've got hits down the length of the ship," the duty engineer said. "We're open to space in several places. We can't take another round like that!"

"That was just the little that came through after the shields fell," the DSO said. "We're doomed if—*missiles inbound!* I've got over 100 missiles inbound, and I can't do anything to stop them!" He switched to the public address system. "*Numerous missiles inbound! All hands brace for shock!* Five seconds! Three...two...one..."

* * * * *

Get "A Gulf in Time" now at: https://www.amazon.com/dp/B0829FLV92

Find out more about Chris Kennedy and "A Gulf in Time" at: https://chriskennedypublishing.com/imprints-authors/chris-kennedy/

* * * * *

Made in the USA
Monee, IL
08 September 2021